Comin' Across Grace

Ashley Halil

DEDICATION

For my husband, Don, who spent way too many date nights talking about the trials and tribulations of Grace.

ACKNOWLEDGEMENTS

I would like to give my love and appreciation to my wonderful husband, Don, and my beautiful children, Savannah, Trip, Cole and Piper for supporting me in this project. They jumped in to help around the house and understood when dinner was late due to the fact that I was immersed in a world far from home.

A special thank you to my brother, Bert. He not only encouraged me to "just finish the book," but is also responsible for the whimsical cover art. He amazes me daily with his creativity, and I aspire to be like him.

I would like to express my gratitude to my parents, Van & Sandra, and my brother, Boyce, for taking the time to read my book. They filled me with positivity and the courage to let my little book out into the world.

Thank you to Dana Jackson, who brought me to tears when she told me she liked the book. I respect her and the job she has done for me. She knocked on many doors which would never have been opened to me.

Thank you to Willy Mathis, my editor and coach. He supported me as I struggled to put the pieces together and always had a Zen way of walking me through to the next chapter. Then, he polished the book as only a good editor can.

Finally, much thanks to Shari Thanner, my partner in writing. She traveled the journey along side of me as a fellow writer. I'm grateful for a friend who understands the struggle of getting the novel from your heart and head onto the page.

1 BEETLES CAN BE THE ANSWER TO YOUR PRAYERS

Is life not giving you what you hope for? Is sadness weighing down upon your heart? Is true love evading you? Is there someone in your life who is facing an illness? Prayer can help. Let me lift up your burdens to the almighty Father. Let me be a voice raising your plea to God. For only $5.00 a day, I will pray for you seven times. That means for just $35 a week, there are 49 prayers floating to Heaven just for you! Believe in the power of prayer. If you email me today, I'll give you an extra prayer at no charge. That makes 50 prayers -- all for you!

I know it might sound crazy to some people, but to others it makes perfect sense. They send their PayPal payment to me each week for my prayers. I pray for their getting job promotions, cancer cures, lottery winnings, and engagement rings. I pray for lost items, dying relatives and smaller prison sentences. You name it, and I've prayed for it.

I pray with my whole heart and soul — after I've received the payment, that is. I have a schedule for my prayers. I stick to it as best as I can. Only sometimes do I have to double up on prayers for a day. Something inside me feels that if the prayers are spaced out throughout the day, they may do the job a little better.

Some folks might wonder who would actually send money for prayers. I wonder the same thing about those people who send money to Facebook for imaginary gifts, or for those who send money to organizations helping stray dogs, when children with AIDS are living in boxes in Africa! I think about those women in fancy cities who buy $3,000 purses and then give 'em away a season later, just because they're out of style. Doesn't thirty-five dollars a week for daily prayers to God sound alright now?

I do feel a little bit bad about what I'm doing — not really "guilty" — just sometimes, a feeling creeps up on me. It's a feeling way off in the back of my stomach that quietly gnaws at my soul. I know charging money for a prayer might be a sin. I'm just figurin' that if my intentions are good, maybe I'll be in the clear. If I wadn't prayin, the bills would pile up. So here I am.

I always knew, even when I was little, I had the good Lord's ear. Everybody in town should know it by now. If somebody in church gets sick, I offer to lay my hands on 'em and pray. Sometimes they're quick prayers and sometimes they take longer than a revival. More times than not, those same people get to feelin' better within a day or two.

A few years back, Reverend Sanders needed money to patch up the steeple, which had been a part of the church since 1928. It's a beautiful tower to look up at, but time had took its toll. When it rained hard for a coupla' days, water poured into the sanctuary, due to the cracks in the steeple. He had to call in a guy from a few counties over, who specialized in preservin' old buildings. He told Reverend Sanders it was gonna' cost $14,938. That's about more money than we get in the collection plate in a year!

The Reverend asked the congregation to pray hard, right after he got the estimate for the repair. He knew it was gonna' take mighty special prayers to get that kind of money. I got down on my knees for this one, seeing how worried Reverend Sanders was. This wasn't an ordinary prayer request. Also, I have a special place in my heart for that church building, seein' as how my parents married there, and I was baptized there. That's also where my momma and daddy spent their last church service before being laid in the cemetery out back. I prayed every day for what seemed like forever as Reverend Sanders all but begged the congregation to dig deep down into their pockets and give extra for our steeple. After church each week, Mrs. Whipple counted out the money in the collection baskets. After a month, they only had $87.59 more than they started with.

That's when I took to prayin' in the church each and ev'ry morning. I wanted to be as close to God as I could, so he would hear my prayers. After about a week of church prayin', I began to see this was another true test from God. But that's when the miracle happened, right there in the church.

It was Sunday morning, and gettin' colder outside. Everyone was bundled up in the sanctuary, because Reverend Sanders had decided to cut the electric bill in order to save money. The children were snugglin' up to their parents, and the grown-ups were rubbin' their hands together for warmth, as the choir filed into their pews. Reverend Sanders made his procession up the aisle and stepped up to his pulpit. *Towerin' behind him, the steeple rose up high — right at the front of the sanctuary — as if directin' our attention straight up to Heaven above. Reverend Sanders looked at his watch and then over his shoulder. He gave Mr. Bartlett the nod, to let him know it was time to start ringin' the church bell. The bell sits high up inside the steeple. Everyone in town could hear it ringin' on Sunday mornings — remindin' 'em that Sunday is the Lord's day and makin' 'em feel guilty if they wasn't sittin' in church.*

As the bell started ringin' that morning, we could all hear a few small poppin' sounds. Then those few small poppin' sounds built up into loud poppin' sounds, like my cousin Jake was firin' his BB gun at a milk carton. Reverend Sanders paused and eyeballed the congregation for the troublemaker who was disruptin' his service. Right then, I noticed the choir glancin' up over their heads into the steeple. As the noise got louder, it became clear the clatter was comin' from up there! They stared straight up, tryin' to figure out what was makin' the commotion. Before any of us could make sense of what was happenin', a huge gust of warm air came shootin' down that steeple and right into the church. At first, the Reverend's notecards flew from the podium and fluttered all around the church, landin' in the aisles and on the pews. Then, as the gush of air moved forward, everyone's bulletins started skitterin' to the floor. Every single one of the candles in the sanctuary blew out. That wind was so strong, everyone's hair started blowin' back from their faces, like we was standin' in front of a big fan!

That's when it started — the panic at Eden Baptist Church. At first, everyone thought the Holy Spirit had descended down among us. Mrs. Marker was sittin' in the front row, where she sat every Sunday, for as long as I've

4

been in church. *She dropped down on her knees and started singin' "Swing Low, Sweet Chariot." Her brother, Boot, raised up his hands in the air and started yellin', "I'm here, Lord!" Reverend Sander's toupee had been blown forward to the front of his face and was hangin' lopsided over his forehead. I could only see one of his eyes from under that pouf of brown hair, but it was as big as a saucer! We all looked around and held our breath, just waitin' to see what was comin' next.*

I don't think we were quite expectin' what did come. The breeze from the Holy Spirit suddenly turned into the sulfur-laden smell of hell! Our sanctuary, which usually had an odor of old choir books and pine cleaner, now smelled like the depths of Satan's belly. And that's when the praisin' turned into hysteria. Reverend Sanders had preached about Armageddon to us many times. We all knew God was goin' to have it out with Satan. Since it seemed they were both in our church, we just figured that prophesied time had arrived.

I have wondered before about the Second Coming. Wondered where I would be and what I would be doin'. I remember sittin' there thinkin' that church was probably a safe place to be durin' a time like this. That was until everyone started runnin' out of the building like it was burnin' down! A feverish ruckus took over and the whole congregation — myself included — began barrelin' toward the doors. We all gathered outside in the parking lot and just stood there with our eyes floatin' back and forth between Heaven and Hell. After a few minutes, nothing happened. Outside, all seemed just like it was supposed to be, which was a little puzzlin'. Nothing was wrong at all. The birds was still chirpin' and the sun was still shinin'. And no matter what any of us might have been fearin', there was no horsemen comin' from any direction.

After some time passed, Reverend Sanders took a few of the men back inside to investigate. As they walked into the sanctuary, they saw Mr. Bartlett standing by the bell rope in terror. He stood frozen in place, paralyzed from fear. The men noticed beetles crawling in his hair and on his shirt. Reverend Sanders called for a flashlight, and when he pointed it up into the steeple, he saw it was swarmin' with millions o' some kind of beetles! It was such a weird sight, that Deacon James actually muttered, "Holy shit!" right in the Lord's house.

Bud, our town exterminator, was called in that very day. Had he been in church like he was supposed to be on a Sunday morning, the Reverend wouldn't have had to track him down at the motel off Route 3. Seems he'd tied on a few at Lucky's Bar and couldn't make it home. When he got to the church with his blood-shot eyes and bangin' headache, he said that he ain't ever see anything like these beetles before. So Reverend Sanders called in an entomologist from the college. That's what they call people who study bugs. That fella' was some kind of happy when he crawled into the steeple and saw the beetles. After collectin' a few in a jar and makin' a phone call back to the university, he told the Reverend all about them.

"Bombardier Beetles," he explained, "are part of the Carabidae family. They're usually ground beetles that live in the woods under logs. Never in all of my years of study have I ever seen a colony this big or known of any to habitate within a man-made structure such as this. It is quite remarkable, really."

He researched for days tryin' to find an explanation, but he came up with nothing, nothing scientific, anyway. Of course, I knew the reason. It was my prayers that did it. We might not have even noticed the beetles in the steeple, if it weren't for the fact these beetles are something pretty special.

According to the professor, they have a mixture of gases in their belly that heats up when they get scared. When this happens, they make a poppin' sound and this stinky gas squirts out everywhere, so's to scare off whatever is thinkin' about eating 'em. That bell ringin' was just enough to scare those little guys silly! They started poppin' and spewin' that heated gas all over the place. It wadn't the second comin', but it was enough to get the attention of everyone in church that Sunday mornin'. They were our own little miracle.

The entomologist asked if he could study the beetles, along with a team from the university. Reverend Sanders said he'd like to help, but the steeple was in need of repair. He explained that havin' a team of men crawlin' around inside the steeple would be mighty dangerous. Then, I got the answer to my prayer. The fella' from the university said they had a grant for $15,000. They offered to turn it over to Eden Baptist Church, if they could hang out and do their study in the steeple for six weeks. Reverend told them as long as they didn't interfere with Sunday services, Wednesday choir practices, or Bible study, they had a deal.

Reverend Sanders started off the next church service by sayin' he wanted to preach about something real special. I wondered about how he was goin' to work those beetles into his sermon. I knew there was only one time in the Bible that beetles was talked about. That was in Leviticus 11. In that verse, the Lord spoke to Moses and told him the children of Israel could eat beetles. I held my breath, hopin' this wasn't where Reverend Sanders was goin'. I didn't think he wanted his flock to have a beetle buffet, regardless of how overjoyed he was about those bugs up there. I was mighty relieved when he told us to open our bibles to Proverbs 15:8.

"The LORD," declared Reverend Sanders, "detests the sacrifice of the wicked, but the prayer of the upright pleases him."

7

Reverend Sanders spent the next hour talkin' about God answerin' our little church's prayer, because we was upright. Apparently, he didn't see Sam Springer who was slumped over in the third row, droolin' as he quietly snored.

Reverend Sanders took the extra $62.00 that was left over from the grant and had a special stepping stone made for the prayer garden. I still get chills when I see the bombardier beetle made out of concrete and colored glass.

It wadn't too long after that that I got my idea for the internet prayer service. Happy Meadows Trailer Estate was in dire straits. Since Mamma and Daddy died, I've tried to keep it up the way they did. I waited tables at night, tryin' to make some extra cash; but that didn't work out so well. I knew I needed more money, but I wasn't sure how I was goin' to make enough to pay for everything that needed payin' for. No matter what you might think, trailer parks ain't cheap!

One evenin', I was watching 48 Hours, and they started talkin' about internet scams. That's when the idea hit me. Don't get me wrong, though, I ain't scammin' nobody. It's just I saw how many people search the internet every day for answers to the problems in their lives. I figured I might as well jump in and help give them some answers . . . for a price, that is. 'Bout that time, I got an email from Patsy, the church secretary. She was sendin' me the prayer request for the week. That's when sellin' my prayers hit me.

So here I am. I make a pretty good livin' off my prayers. Enough to keep the trailer park runnin' and still manage to eat. I start off each day by prayin'. I make sure to pray for every one of my clients seven times a day, to avoid false advertising.

You'll have to excuse me. It's now 10:30 — time to pray for Cindy in Humboldt, Kansas.

Our heavenly Father, please forgive my sins. Also, please forgive me for not going to church this morning. I knew that hittin' that snooze button on the alarm wasn't right, but I sure was enjoyin' my bed. I am calling to you for your daughter Cindy in Humboldt, Kansas. She is the one I told you about just this morning. Remember? The one who works at that drugstore. She is asking that you help her win $1000. Please look down upon her in the upcoming Bible Extravaganza Parade. Her Uncle Ricky, who owns Mayfair Drugstore, sponsors a float every year. This year, he asked Cindy to build the float representin' his store. She does have an eye for fashion, accordin' to her Aunt Nancy. Anyway, if she does a good job and wins for her creation of Jesus, your Son, in the Garden of Gethsemane, she'll get $1000. That's a lot of money. She says she is gonna' use it to relocate to Florida. Anyway, please look kindly upon her as the judges are judging the floats. Help her to win, if it be your will. In the name of your precious son. Amen.

There, that should do it for now. Sometimes my prayers are a little longer than others. I always begin by asking God to forgive my own sins. It always seemed to me He would hear you a little clearer if your soul is clean and bright. I also try to never sound too demandin' about what it is I'm askin' for. In the end, it's all about His will being done, anyhow. I do believe that. Nothin' can happen unless He wants it to happen. He's smarter than we are about what's good for us and what ain't. I always explain this to my potential clients. It wouldn't matter if a whole city prayed for you, day in and day out, if that wasn't the best thing for you and wasn't his will, it wouldn't happen. Before I even accept payment for services rendered, I always send a contract to my customers. I spell out for them right there that I am promisin' to pray only. I can't affect the outcome in any way. I am only a voice liftin' up a plea to the Almighty. Whether or not that plea is answered, that is out of my hands. With that off my chest, I sit back and chuckle knowin' that, with my track record, most of those prayers are already on the way to bein' answered.

2 CINDY FROM HUMBOLDT, KANSAS

"That'll be $2.15, Mrs. Blue," said Cindy.

"Here you go, dear. I figured I ought to have an extra pair of scissors on hand when we start our Women's Circle Meeting at church. We're working on the float, you know. Of course, I can't tell you anything about it, since you *are* competing against us; but I can say that it *is* quite a masterpiece. Many items from the women's bazaar have come in handy."

"I'm glad to hear it. The parade will be here before we know it. Good luck to you."

"Thank you. You, too."

As Mrs. Blue walked out of the door, Cindy took a deep breath and grabbed the notebook from under the cash register. She began flipping through the pages of designs for the Garden of Gethsemane. She had dreamed of designing a float for as long as she'd been watching the parades, which had been her whole life.

11

The Bible Extravaganza Parade is the only parade in the whole country that showcases Bible stories and the people contained within them. Every year, floats stretch down Main Street depicting lions, burning bushes, small men in trees and prostitutes. This was the one time of the year someone could *really* stand out in this small town. The rest of the year, you might as well just stop time. It's like the weather is the only thing that doesn't forget to change. Of course, with the changing weather come tornados. Tornados plagued and terrified Cindy since before she was even born.

Cindy's mother, Jo, short for Josephine, was eight months and six days pregnant when a twister came tearing through the town. Jo had been at Lou's Beauty Salon getting the perm. She had long, straight, auburn hair that swung back and forth as she walked. But now that she was about to become a mother, an adult responsible for another human being, she decided a more adult hair style was in order. Lou had half of Jo's hair set in curlers when the sirens began to wail. Everyone in Humboldt knows what to do when that siren wails. Tornados are a common occurrence in the Midwest, but "common" doesn't mean predictable. So everyone in Lou's gathered in the bathroom. There was Jo, Lou, and two other hairdressers huddled together, as the water in the toilet bowl began to swish around. They heard the roaring and knew that this one was coming close. Of course, this wasn't anything new to anyone who had grown up in Humboldt, or most places in Kansas for that matter. However, when they heard the windows blowing out of the front of the salon, they realized they were in for it. *This one was right on top of them.*

Jo had seen *The Wizard of Oz* too many times to count. The scene came to mind where Dorothy is thrown on her bed. She begins to see all the things from the farm floating by, as she sits in the center of the tornado. Jo immediately thought of the twister picking up the hair dryers and the little glass canister filled with blue liquid and combs. In her mind, she could see them swirling around, along with the hair cuttings that were lying on the floor. What she *didn't* see was the brick wall collapsing on top of her and her friends. She didn't imagine the toilet tank ripping from the wall and crashing against her, or the four by six beam falling on top of her, or the fact that there would be no munchkin skipping toward her with a giant lollipop.

After only minutes, the twister had pulled up into itself, and there were actually patches of blue sky. The birds, although nervous, began to chirp. The siren grew silent and the phones began to ring all over the city, as friends and family called to "check in" on each other. Everyone was fine, it seemed — everyone except those unfortunate few who were gossiping and laughing in Lou's Beauty Salon. The tornado had sprung from a farm in a neighboring county and landed directly on top of Lou's.

It was "quick and vicious," according to Mary Mayweather on the evening news. "Yes, folks, it was vicious enough to take the life of one Josephine Sink. However, by some miracle, her unborn child was born healthy and unharmed."

On that same news broadcast, Lou was interviewed. With wide eyes, she told the town of the horrible experience. "Suddenly, the rumble was so loud, I began to get scared. Then, the wall just fell! I was under the edge of the counter. I got these scrapes and bruises . . . but other than that, me and the other two girls were fine. My heart stopped when I looked over at Jo. I knew she wasn't breathing. The fire trucks and ambulances arrived minutes later and delivered her sweet little baby. I sobbed when I heard her little cry. They took the baby right away. Then there was Jo. Her long brown hair hung over one shoulder, while the other side was curlers. I thought, *she would look mighty odd in the casket with half of her hair straight.* So I grabbed the rollers and finished her perm right then and there, as tears were streaming down my face. She looked beautiful when they zipped up her body bag."

Cindy began thumbing through pages of sketches, looking for pictures depicting the float she dreamt up. In her mind's eye, there was Jesus, praying on the front of the float, surrounded by flowers. Peter, James and John would lie towards the back of the float under the shade of olive trees. With a $200 budget, Cindy had to be thrifty and creative. Uncle Ricky gave her all the returned or damaged merchandise that had been piling up in the back store room. She could use anything there at no loss to her budget. Making something out of nothing was a talent she had developed early on in her life.

It started when she was quite young. First, she made a mother and father out of her Aunt Nancy and Uncle Ricky. They decided before they ever married that kids were not something they wished for. Many can't understand that. Nancy's mother never understood it.

"Who will take care of you when you're old?" she would argue. "Who will carry on the memories you make here on earth? Aren't we all meant for procreation?"

Nancy used to laugh. "Momma, this is *my* life. You just want grandchildren, I know. But Ricky and I are going to travel the world. We're going to see things this little town has never even heard of. It's *our* decision."

She hated to see her mother upset, but that was just the way it was going to be. Nancy figured that sooner or later, her mother would have to get over it.

But when Jo, Ricky's sister, was killed, their lives changed. Ricky was Cindy's only living relative. The father of the baby was a secret to everyone in town. Jo used to tell people the father had ridden into Humboldt on a black stallion, and after one beautiful night together, "he left in a trail of dust to battle evil." Then Jo would usually add he promised to return when all "evil was smited." Only Ricky knew the true story. Jo had made a road trip with a few girlfriends to Topeka for a weekend of big city fun. They had met a group of soldiers who were on leave from Fort Riley. All the girls made lots of wonderful memories for themselves that weekend. And Jo, along with her one-night stand soldier, made Cindy. She didn't even get the soldier's last name . . . on account of the fact her friend Renee was so ashamed about the entire night of foolin' around, she demanded they all sneak out of the hotel and hit the road before the sun even rose.

Jo was shaken by the fact she was having a baby out of wedlock, but she thought *to hell with it.* She knew deep in her heart she was going to have a little girl; and in her mind, that little girl was already her best friend. She pictured them making chocolate chip cookies together, crying over romantic movies, shopping, and snuggling each night in bed. Jo wasn't scared about having a baby. She was excited about having a best friend.

Ricky had never quite understood his sister. Her head was always in the clouds. He tried to talk her back down to earth, when she told him "the best news of all times," as she had put it. She wasn't going to have *anything* but smiles and congratulations.

"If you're not going to celebrate with me," she told Ricky, "then go hang out with those old biddies down at the diner. I'm happy and my little girl is going to be a princess!"

With that, Ricky threw his hands up in defeat and did all he could to make Jo's pregnancy wonderful. He was even putting together the most wonderful gift basket of sundries from the drug store—diapers, bottles, and even baby aspirin—when the tragedy struck.

Ricky and Nancy's plans of traveling the country and spending quiet nights all alone in their home were squashed that very day, like a pesky mosquito on your leg. They immediately took little Cindy home from the hospital, as soon as the doctors had declared her healthy and unharmed.

Tears rolled down Nancy's cheeks, as she held that beautiful baby girl in her arms at Jo's funeral. She stood over Jo's coffin and whispered, "This is your little Princess, Jo. She has your dark hair and your wondrous eyes. I promise we will be good to her. We love you. Go fly with your angels."

Good to her they were, too. Ricky and Nancy often laughed together quietly, thinking back to the foolish days when they actually believed having a child would *certainly* be a burden. This child was the blessing of all blessings. "My little cup of Jo"—that's what Uncle Ricky would call Cindy every once in a while, when he saw her gazing into space, just like her mother had. They both appeared to be a thousand miles away . . . far away from their room, far away from their home, and far away from Humboldt.

Cindy dreamt, but she was realistic about reaching her dreams. She was all that Uncle Ricky and Aunt Nancy could ever hope for in a child.

That's why moving to Florida was a precarious situation for Cindy. Although she loved Ricky and Nancy, she knew something was waiting for her in Florida. Just what, she wasn't sure. She only knew that the sound of the ocean often came to her as she was drifting off to sleep. When she was younger, she didn't know what the sound was—only that is was relaxing, as she closed her eyes and let her mind turn off. She didn't realize it was Florida calling her every day, until she turned sixteen.

Shortly after her sixteenth birthday, Cindy came home after school just like she did any other day. She made a peanut butter and banana sandwich, grabbed a coke and headed to the den to start her algebra homework. *God,* how she hated algebra! She figured she would finish it first and work on her poem for English afterwards. Her motto was: "Get the worst part over with first." But even as she wrote down the first problem, her mind wandered. *Imagine, only two more years of math,* she thought. Then, she would be free to do whatever she wanted to do. She could continue with her schooling, as Uncle Ricky and Aunt Nancy expected her to, or she could bolt and see the world. Numbers would mean nothing more than dates, times and money. Slope, functions and variables would be a thing of the past.

Now, Nancy had brought Cindy up in the First Baptist Church of Humboldt, and talking to God was something the church encouraged. Pastor Terry used to say, "Talk to God like he's your best friend. Talk to God like he's your mother or father. Talk to God as if he is your lover—your husband or wife. Because he is *all* of those things and more. Don't go a single hour without stopping to talk to him. He never goes a single hour without talking to you. If you listen, you'll hear him and see him in everything around you."

This mini-sermon swam back into Cindy's mind, as she sat there doing her homework that day. She *did* say her prayers daily. She asked God to forgive her for her sins, to bless her friends and family, and she thanked him for everything he had given her. That was the extent of their closeness, though. In the scheme of school and friends, she neglected the "hourly chats with the Lord." However, as she sat contemplating her life, instead of algebra, she decided to take a few minutes to talk to God.

"Hi, God. It's me, Cindy. I guess you probably know that, though. I only have two years left of high school." She paused and pictured the kind face of Jesus staring at her and shaking his head, as if recognition was sinking in.

"I think you did a good job making a town like Humboldt. It's a real nice place to live."

Then she wondered whether or not she should mention that if the tornadoes vanished, it would be even better. She decided to save that for another time. She didn't want anything to come between God and the reason for her prayer. Better not to criticize someone who you are about to ask for a favor.

"I really want to go and explore your beautiful world, though." Cindy smiled, hoping God accepted flattery.

"I feel like you've got a plan for me, Jesus. One that takes me further than Highway 169. I just am wondering where that is. Dear Lord, if you see fit to share with me your plan, I sure would be happy. I try to picture myself years from now. I just can't see where I am or what I'm doing."

Her prayer was suddenly interrupted by the phone ringing.

"Hello."

"Hi, baby," said Ricky. "I was just watching the news here at the store, and the weather looks like it is gonna' get bad. Why don't you come on over. Just in case. I don't want you there by yourself."

Nobody had to tell Cindy twice when it came to storms. Where there was a storm, there could be a tornado. And the store had a basement that was indestructible.

"I'll leave now," Cindy said. "See you soon."

She grabbed her backpack and sandwich and headed out the door. As she walked to the bug—the nickname she'd given her iridescent blue Volkswagen Beetle—the wind began to pick up. It swept her long, wavy hair up into the air and in front of her big, brown eyes, momentarily blurring her vision. And as the wind picked up, so did her heart rate. She didn't like this. The sky was taking on that greenish cast that always came with tornado weather. Pushing the hair back from her eyes, she scanned the sky. There was nothing on the immediate horizon. She quickly climbed into the bug and headed for the drug store. Cindy kept watching the sky and the angry looking tree branches overhead, as she drove a little faster.

After driving just a mile or so, Cindy realized she hadn't finished her prayer. In an effort to take her mind off of the increasingly dark sky, she decided to quickly finish.

"Please give me a sign, dear Lord. Let me know where I'm headed, so I can work to get there. I promise to be a faithful and kind Christian, dear Lord. Thank you for taking this time with me. Please help me to get to the store fast. In Jesus Christ's name, I pray. Amen."

Suddenly, a brochure flew from the sky and landed smack dab in the middle of her windshield. She swerved more than she normally would have, since her nerves were on edge. As she righted the car, Cindy looked at the glossy piece of paper, colorfully splayed with white sand and a beautiful blue ocean. Across the top were the words: *Come visit the Sunshine State — where the ocean meets paradise!*

She felt a jolt of excitement, as the brochure blew off the windshield and down the street. That was it. It was her sign. *It had to be.* Her stomach fluttered with butterflies, as she pictured herself walking along the beach in a pink sarong blowing in the breeze.

It started raining and her mind was jolted back to the present — *only a few more minutes until I reach the store*, she thought. As excited as she was about the possibility that Florida was her future, the terror of a twister took over. She pressed the gas pedal harder, turned the radio down and cracked the window. No sirens yet. That was a good thing. As she turned down 1st Street, she spotted the store. There were plenty of parking spaces out front. She pulled in and quickly made her way in. Just as she opened the door, the sirens began to sound.

Cindy could feel it, just as she always did. Her lungs began to close. She opened her mouth, trying to get a breath of air, but nothing came in. With shaking hands, she willed herself to stay calm; but as the sirens continued to blare, her throat felt smaller and smaller. She looked around with wide, watering brown eyes. She saw Uncle Ricky heading towards her with a brown paper bag.

"It's okay, Cindy. Here, baby. Put this over your mouth, now. Take a deep breath for me."

As she began to attempt a breath, her eyebrows shot up over the bag in a question.

"She's here, baby. Aunt Nancy is down in the basement already. Come on."

He locked the store's front door and held Cindy around the waist, as he led her down the steps. Nancy was at their side quicker than a blink. She sat Cindy down on the little sofa and began to rub her back.

"Just breathe. now. That's a good girl. You're here, safe and sound. Nothing can hurt you down here. Just relax."

Cindy could feel her throat obeying Aunt Nancy. *Finally*, she felt a bit of air reach her lungs. She closed her eyes and concentrated on the bag, on Aunt Nancy's soft hands on her back, and on the sound of Uncle Ricky's breathing. She finally felt herself returning to her body. Pulling the bag away from her mouth, she looked at Ricky with a mixture of tears and embarrassed laughter.

"Will I ever stop this?" she asked.

"You'll stop one day, honey. Your strength will come."

"Some days," she replied, "I think the only way to beat this is to move. Get out of the path of the crazy twisters. Move someplace far away, where they don't even *have* tornado sirens. Someplace where the sun is always shining—like Florida!"

Ricky and Nancy looked at each other with dread in their eyes. Cindy saw it . . . the hurt at even the *thought* of not being close to her. She was sorry as soon as she'd said it.

"You know, in Florida they have hurricanes. That's a lot like tornados. In California they have earthquakes. No place is perfect, baby," said Nancy.

"I know. You're right," Cindy said. She figured it would be easier to just drop it and let the subject rest for now.

She knew she still had a few years left until graduation. That was plenty of time to gradually wear them down and assure them she'd never *really* leave them. They were her parents, like it or not.

The tornado that hit that day did *some* damage to Humboldt, but mostly it just took out its aggression on trees and power lines. Although one trailer, on the outskirts of town, was moved about five feet from its previous spot on concrete blocks. When the double siren sounded to let the town know it was safe to get out and about, Cindy, Ricky and Nancy peered out the front door to survey the damage. Everything on Main Street looked okay. The sky was beginning to clear.

"Do you want to stay here in the store? I just got a shipment of nail polish that needs to be stocked. I'll give you a few to try," offered Ricky.

"I'd love some new nail polish, but I've got algebra homework."

"Are you going to be okay to drive home, sweetheart?"

"I'm fine now that the sky is clearing. I'll see you both at home later."

Cindy headed out to the bug and brushed the leaves from the windshield with her hand. She drove through town, checking to see how much havoc the tornado had caused. There was hardly anything. She flipped on the radio. According to the correspondent at the National Weather Center, the tornado had actually been one of many that swept across the Midwest. Twisters had been spotted not only in Kansas, but also in Oklahoma and Arkansas. They had skipped across several states, leaving a path of minor destruction.

The tornado that hit Humboldt had moved many miles before it died out. On the outskirts of town, Cindy noticed a little more damage. As she turned left onto County Road 2, she thought again about Florida. God had heard her, just like Pastor Terry promised. She knew then and there that something wonderful was waiting for her in the Sunshine State.

3 SHE OPENS HER ARMS TO THE POOR AND EXTENDS HER HANDS TO THE NEEDY

Although I do charge for my prayers, I think God expects us to give back to those who can't afford to pay nothin'. "She opens her arms to the poor and extends her hands to the needy." — Proverbs 31:20. I memorized that verse in vacation Bible school, when I was just a little thing. It always stuck with me, though. Back then, I took everything real literal. I remember walkin' up to Drunk Joe, who always slept outside the post office, and standin' over him with my arms held wide. I stood there for a good ten minutes or so, til' finally he opened his eyes.

"What the hell you doin', girl? Get on away from here!" he snapped.

I still remember that sour smell of old alcohol mingled with body odor and urine. I kept myself from breathin' through my nose, so I wouldn't have to smell him, but I kept my feet planted. I bent down and reached out my hand to him.

"Are you retarded or somethin'? Go on! Get."

"Don't be scared, Mr. Joe. I'm just extendin' my hand to the needy."

"Unless you got a bottle in that hand, you best get it out of my face."

He started to look angry. I figured I should go find another needy person. Although things didn't go right with Drunk Joe, I never did forget that verse. That's why,` when I got an email from Drew in the Ware State Prison over in Georgia, I decided to pray for him at no charge. Now, I know what you're probably thinkin'. Couldn't you find someone else to be charitable to besides some criminal? When he first emailed me, I thought the same thing. I'll own up to that. But after prayin' on it, I took out my Bible for some answers. I found it in Leviticus, chapter twenty-four, verse twelve. "And they put him in custody, till the will of the Lord should be clear to them."

I guessed that maybe I was gonna' be the one who made God's will clear. So, I answered Drew's email. I told him I would pray for him, and I understood he couldn't pay me nothin'. I took to emailin' Drew and prayin' for him as often as I could. It took a few more emails, until Drew told me what he had done. I have to admit, I was real happy he wasn't a rapist or murderer or anything like that. I don't know that I would have felt real good about prayin' for that kind of man.

Drew and I send emails to each other on a regular schedule, now. I email him on Mondays and Thursdays, and I always know I'm gonna' get emails from him on Tuesdays and Fridays. I pray every day that God helps him repent for his sins. I pray for the day he knows God's will is for him to be a good, faithful man who tries hard not to sin.

4 DREW FROM WARE STATE PRISON

Drew Nalley almost got away with it. He was so close, he could almost *feel* the cash in his hands. Just a few more jobs and he could nearly *see* himself reclining on a beach with the sun shining on his face and a cold piñā colada touching his lips. Instead, he was in the Ware State Prison sitting on a cool metal bench with a lukewarm bottle of water to his lips. When he pondered his scheme — which he did at least once a day — he knew *exactly* what he had done wrong. There was one error that brought everything crashing down on his head...literally.

Growing up in Georgia, Drew had seen his share of poverty. His family owned fifteen acres of farming land that had been passed down over the years. At one time, there had been eighty-seven acres. However, through hard times, the family had sold off bits and pieces. When his grandfather passed away, the land was passed on to Drew's father, Henry, who had big plans. He had known what to do with the land for many years, and patiently waited for his time to take over the family farm. When that time came, he immediately dug up all the peanut plants that currently spread along the farm land, and then took the family savings—which wasn't much—and purchased peach trees and Vidalia onion seeds.

One night, many years before, while sitting on the front porch of his worn-down farm house, Henry popped open his fourth beer and looked towards the sky. He had worked hard planting peanuts that day and decided to rest for a few minutes before dinner. His wife was making fried boloney and cheese sandwiches for dinner with home-made onion rings. Henry had stopped at the market for his beer earlier in the week and on the way out, also grabbed a basket full of peaches. They were in season and he couldn't resist the sweet smell of them.

So, this particular night, Henry's wife was making a peach pie out of those very peaches for dessert. As he gazed at the sky and sipped on his beer, an idea came floating to him in the breeze. "It was brilliant," Henry would later say. He realized, while smelling the onion rings and the peach pie, that by planting the Vidalia onion plants at the base of the peach trees, the onions would be even sweeter. That is, the sweet flavor of the peaches would seep into his Vidalias. And he would have the best, most sought after onions in the county!

Drew remembered helping his father plant the peach trees. He also vividly recalled their bending over and placing the onion seeds all around the tree. Then, they spent months watering and fertilizing. Henry purchased a new lock for the gate at the end of the dirt road leading to their farm. And once he snapped that lock shut on the gate, he turned around and swore Drew to secrecy.

"Boy, don't you never tell no one what we did. *You hear?* This is our family secret. This is how you're going to get that new rifle you want. Folks are going to be comin' from counties all over Georgia for our Vidalias."

Mention of the rifle was all Drew needed for incentive. His lips were sealed. Finally, harvest time came. The onions were ready to be harvested a few months before the peaches. Henry brought his wife and Drew out to the orchard. He had a small TV-tray with a beer and two glasses of iced tea on it. Next to the drinks were a knife and a cutting board. He ushered them over and smiled proudly.

"This is going to be our future *right here*. Mark this day in your memory." Henry walked to the closest peach tree and dug down with his bare hands into the dirt below. He pulled out an onion and brushed off the dirt. Holding it up to the sky, he smiled.

"Ain't that a beauty? Not a flaw on it."

He placed it reverently on the cutting board and sliced it in half. Peeling off the outer layer, Henry sliced a few pieces, and handed one to Drew and one to his wife.

"Take a bite of our miracle!"

They all bit into the crunchy onion. There was a moment of excitement followed by a moment of consideration. They looked at each other for reactions,

29

each wondering if their assessment was the same as the other. Finally, Henry's smile faded, and he swallowed.

"Something must be wrong. Maybe that one wasn't planted close enough to the tree. It don't taste no different from any other Vidalia.

Drew nodded. "I'll get another one, Pops."

Drew went to another tree and dug up one that was right against the trunk of the peach tree. He ran back to Henry and put the onion on the cutting board. After their second taste test, they tried twelve more . . . *all* with the same results. Although the Vidalias were fine, as far as Vidalias go, they were nothing special.

Henry swallowed hard and looked around at his land. He looked at his wife's face, who stared back at him with a look of pity. Then he looked at Drew's face. There were tears welling up in his eyes.

"Ain't nothing to cry about, boy," Henry said. "We might not have the best Vidalia's in Georgia, but we can still sell 'um. The peaches will be ready to harvest in six weeks or so. Hopefully, we'll make enough to get through till next year. We might still have a little money left over for that rifle."

Six weeks later, the peaches were plump and fragrant. The smell was almost sickeningly sweet, as Henry walked through the trees. He decided to pluck a few to have with dinner. This would be the first time they had tasted the peaches. He hoped there would be enough to clear a decent profit.

Henry laid the peaches on the kitchen counter. "Brought these in for dinner," he said to his wife.

She nodded. "I'll cut them up. Dinner is ready. Call Drew in."

They sat at the old wooden table and begin passing around bowls filled with peas, collards, biscuits and peaches. Drew looked at the peaches excitedly. He loved peaches. He grabbed his fork and plunged it into a slice of peach and popped it into his mouth. He chewed a few times and looked at his father with big worried eyes. He spit the peach into his napkin.

"What did you do that for?" Henry asked.

Drew's father grabbed a slice of peach and ate it. He promptly spit his slice out, as well.

"What is it?" his wife asked.

"Onions," he answered. "They taste like *onions*. They're *terrible*. Like eating a slice of juicy, fuzzy onion."

"Surely they aren't all like that," she answered.

They trailed out of the house to the peach trees. They took turns plucking peaches off one tree and then another. Sure enough, every single one of them tasted like onions.

Drew always pinpointed that moment as the moment when he vowed he would have money, *no matter what*. And he wasn't going to waste his time on this old farm growing onion-tasting peaches. He was going to get the hell out and make the kind of money that would let him buy a whole arsenal of rifles.

So, when Drew turned eighteen, he said goodbye to his parents and headed to the big city of Atlanta. He never did get his rifle, but he got a much better weapon—good looks. He had grown into an attractive young man, and he used his looks to his advantage whenever he could. He quickly found that a wink and a smile could get him a better tip at the club where he bartended. It also got him quite a few phone numbers — phone numbers of women who didn't mind a night here or there with a virile young stud.

As the bar filled up one Friday night, Drew noticed a tall, slender blond woman gazing at him from a table by the dance floor. He locked eyes with her a few times and finally gave her his famous wink and nodded. He sent one of the waitresses over with a fresh drink and instructions to tell her it was on the house. When that drink was gone, the woman came to the bar and sat down.

"Looks like you need a refill there," Drew said, smiling.

"I do, as a matter of fact, sugar."

He noticed, as he served her another drink, that although she was very pretty, she seemed sad in some way. He noted the wedding ring on her finger, with a very big diamond. Her roots were the same color as the end of her hair and her nails were perfectly manicured. He could almost smell the money. *She's a kept woman,* he thought, *who probably isn't kept happy at all.* These were easy targets for Drew.

He had been in Atlanta for three years, and had made some headway. A string of one-night stands, after which something small was invariably missing each time he left in the morning: a pair of pearl earrings, a twenty-dollar bill from a wallet, even a sterling silver fork. Nothing big enough to arouse suspicion or put an end to his escapades. Sam at the pawn store never asked any questions and paid a fair price for whatever items Drew brought in.

Still, the small amount of money he made at the bar, with the extra income from his ladies, wasn't enough to fulfill Drew. He wanted money for that arsenal. He needed to up his game and shoot for wealthier targets. Judging from the looks of the woman sitting across the bar, she could be a home-run. He poured her two more strong drinks, before he began his flirting in earnest. The bar had slowed down, and there was only an hour until closing.

"So what brings a beautiful girl like you into a bar like this alone?" he asked.

"I'll tell you what *doesn't* bring me in, or *who* doesn't bring me in . . . my *husband*. He doesn't take me to dinner. He doesn't take me shopping. He doesn't take me on vacations. He doesn't take me to the club. He doesn't take me *anywhere*. He's out of town on a hunting trip, so I decided to take *myself* out tonight." Big tears began to drip down her cheeks, leaving a pale streak in her make-up.

Now, being in the field that he was in, Drew knew that tears are a necessary part of most of his trysts. A woman usually had to be upset in order to partake in Drew's services. So he wasn't alarmed. He knew how to handle tears. He pulled a napkin from the bar and walked around to the stool where she sat. He dabbed her cheeks gently and, with the back of his pinky, gently wiped the mascara from under her eyes.

"You look like you could use a hug," he said. He wrapped her in his strong arms and stroked her hair. As she looked up at him, he knew she was hooked.

"Don't cry now, it's going to be alright. You really shouldn't be driving in this condition. Maybe I should call you a cab." He glanced at his watch with a look of concern, and then continued, "Hell, I get off in thirty minutes. If you'll just wait, I'll take you home . . . uh, what's your name?"

She sniffed and managed a slight smile. "Amanda, and that would be nice, Drew," she said as she glanced at his nametag. "Thank you."

Drew finished wiping down the countertops and clocked out. He pulled the chair out for Amanda and took her arm, as they walked to the parking lot. She stumbled to his car as the effects of Drew's heavy-handed drinks continued to do their job. Amanda guided him through Atlanta to a gated neighborhood in one of the wealthiest parts of the city. He began to get excited, as he thought about the bounty he would have after a few hours with Amanda. Her house was the biggest Drew had ever been in. It was all he could do to keep his cool, as they walked through the entryway to a set of steps that gave a nod to the spiral staircase in *Gone with the Wind*.

Amanda took off her heels and attempted to make it up the first few steps. Drew reached out to steady her. "Let me help you there, darlin'. I don't want you falling down." He helped her to the top floor and followed her into the bedroom.

As Drew took in the plush oriental carpet and the antique, four-poster bed that almost reached the ten-foot ceilings, Amanda stared at him. She swayed, as she pointed to the closet.

"Will you help me out of this dress?" she asked.

Drew followed her into the closet and quickly spied a jewelry box sitting on a marble-topped chest of drawers. He also noticed three shelves full of purses sporting the markings of Gucci, Coach or some other high-end designer.

"Sugar?" Amanda asked, as she turned her back to him. "Just unzip the back, will you?"

Drew pulled his eyes away from the treasures and focused on Amanda. Making her happy and putting her at ease was an important part of his ruse. He gently unzipped the dress and slipped it from her shoulders. She turned around and threw her arms around his neck.

"Drew," she slurred, "will you kiss me?"

He happily obliged. "You just make yourself at home, Sugar. I'm going to go to the little girl's room. Don't go anywhere, now." She stumbled to the bathroom.

Drew quickly began going through the jewelry box, carefully selecting pieces that were near the bottom — things that probably hadn't been worn for a while. He slipped these into his jacket pockets, then grabbed a Coach Wallet, an expensive looking scarf, and a wad of cash he found neatly placed on her closet shelf. He had learned not to be too greedy, so he quickly unfolded the cash and only took half of it. *She probably didn't have any idea how much money was there to start with*, he thought.

He zipped up his pockets and turned to make his way back into the bedroom, when he heard the toilet flush. As he rounded the corner, he was struck in the head with the cold, hard barrel of a rifle. Drew's vision suddenly went blurry, and he felt his body hit the rug, which didn't seem as plush as it had before. He could feel the diamond broach in his pocket pressing into his ribs, just as he passed out.

The next thing he knew, Drew was in a police car with his hands cuffed behind his back. Lights were flashing, and he could just make out Amanda, standing on the front porch with a blanket wrapped around her.

A big, burly man in hunting gear stood beside her, talking to seven police men. As he barked out orders, the police men nodded and yes sir'd.

One of the officers got into the car and glanced in the rearview mirror. "I see you're awake now, son. For your sake, you best keep pretending you're out cold. Judge Paley sees you're conscious, and he's liable to do more with that rifle than whack you with it."

Drew obediently shut his eyes and thought, *Shit, shit, shit. What have I done?*

Drew couldn't believe he got four year in Ware State Prison. If only it hadn't been *a judge's* wife, he would have probably gotten away with it. Now, he sat in a cold, damp cell for eighteen hours a day. Luckily, he had been given the chance to complete his GED while behind bars. This allowed him four hours a day to use the computers in the jail. The assignments were pretty easy for him, so he spent the last hour or so surfing the web, at least the sites that weren't blocked because of inappropriate content, like pornography and bomb making. He also spent part of this time emailing Grace, "the prayer lady."

He had stumbled upon her ad and decided to write to her, just for kicks. He had never been to church and wasn't religious at all; but the prisoner in the cell next to his said prayers every night before bed. Even though Drew doubted there was a God, there was something peaceful about hearing that fellow's prayers each night.

He was surprised when he got an email back from the woman. All emails that are sent from the jail are clearly marked, "Sent from a Ware State Prison Inmate." He guessed that if someone was truly religious, they wouldn't have anything to do with a man in prison. Since he had nobody else to communicate with on the outside, he decided to continue the correspondence as long as he could, which he knew wouldn't be long, since he didn't have a penny to pay for her prayer services.

To his surprise, she told him he didn't have to worry about paying her. She told him in her reply she was, "happy to extend her hands to the needy." Drew didn't complain. He was happy to have someone talk to him about something other than packs of cigarettes and plans to escape the jail.

It didn't take him long to get her to open up about her life. He quickly found his charm worked, even when he wasn't face-to-face with a woman. The same techniques still applied. Ask them about themselves. Compliment them. Sound vulnerable and sincere. The words came just as easily on the computer screen as they did from his mouth. Women are always looking for someone to share with them and listen to them.

In the spirit of keeping their relationship interesting, Drew began making up stories about the tragedies and downfalls of his life in prison.

He told her about Lark, a guy who collected every cockroach he found in the prison walls and kept them in a small plastic Country Crock container. Lark would keep collecting until he had filled up the bucket, and then he'd release them into the cell of whoever had pissed him off that week. Drew told Grace he'd been the receiver of the cockroaches *twice*.

He told her about Harry Winston, who stole Drew's fruit every morning at breakfast and threatened to tell the guards that he talked about suicide, if he told on him. Anyone at the prison who mentioned suicide was locked up without blankets or anything that could be harmful for at least a week, or until the prison psychologist had deemed them safe to themselves and others.

Drew painted quite a picture for her about the prison guards who had a back room, where they played poker and drank whisky. He told her that if Officer Manny lost money, he came out as mad as a hornet and often beat the first inmate he saw with his club.

By the time he was done with his stories, he had Grace in the palm of his hand. She told him all about her other clients, names excluded, and all about her life. He began wondering if he could manipulate her as easily as he had been able to manipulate the other women who had crossed his path.

Of course, he always thanked her profusely for giving him hope, happiness, and making the days interesting.

5 ABSOLUTION & STUFF

Sometimes, prayin' for somebody is a little tricky. I just got a new client last week named Arnold. I think he wants me to pray for him, because he is too scared to pray for himself. From what I can tell, it's like if he don't pray himself, he might fly under the radar and the Big Guy might not notice whether or not what he is doing is right or wrong. He isn't askin' for anything other than, in his own words, "absolution from his transgressions." According to catholicstoday.com, that just means forgiveness. I felt it was my duty to tell Arnold I'm not a priest or nothin'. I'm just a regular person. I asked him if that would still work for a Catholic. He said he actually hadn't been to mass since he was twelve, so he wasn't really sure. He is just worried that life is too good right now, and he wants to make sure that things keep goin' the way they're goin'. I know what he means. Sometimes, when my life seems calm, like everything is going my way, I think, "Oh, Lord, what's comin'? Things cain't be this easy, can they?" That's the way I was feelin' right after I fell in love with Wayne Darell.

Not too long ago, I was feelin' pretty lonely. It was hard livin' in the trailer all by myself, with nothin' but the sound of the TV and the computer to fill up the space.

At church that week, Reverend Sanders announced that Polly Snow and Henry Trotter was gonna' get married. He congratulated them and asked all us at church to pray for them, as they got ready to start their lives together. I was thinkin' how nice it would be if I had someone to start my life with too.

So I asked Jesus to send me somebody to share myself with. He must have had a slow morning that day, because he sure took my prayer to heart. Before I knew it, I had three somebodies wanting to be with me. Although I was real thankful for His dedication to my cause, I had to pick just one. The choice seemed real clear.

The first boy sent to me by Jesus was Tim, the lawn man at Happy Lawn Trailer Town. He had been doin' the yards there for going on two years; but the morning after my prayer, he was ridin' by on his lawn mower and, for the first time ever, looked over my way and smiled. Tim ain't ever even so much as looked at me before. I always thought maybe he had somethin' wrong with him, in his head, I mean. His uncle owns the lawn company Tim works for, so when I need somthin' done at Happy Lawn, I give his uncle a call. Then Tim shows up later that day like a ghost . . . in and out without a sound. I asked his uncle about him one day, when he stopped by to check on things around the park. He told me Tim was real shy and didn't talk, but that he was a real hard worker.

So, I was real taken aback when he smiled and waved at me that day. Course, I waved back. When I did, his eyebrows near about jumped under the top of his John Deere baseball cap. He took off the cap, smiled and gave me a big old wave. As he was doin' so, he forgot he was supposed to be steerin' that tractor. He ran right into Mrs. Sullivan's twinkle light rosebush, which was that woman's pride and joy. I must say, that bush was one of my favorite things at Happy Lawn. The roses were white and smelled so sweet when they bloomed. However, at night, when Mrs. Sullivan plugged up the twinkle lights, each rose was a different color. You remember Joseph's coat of many colors? Well this was like Mrs. Sullivan's rose bush of many colors. It would downright make you tear up when it was in full bloom.

Tim knew, as well as I did, that when he hit that bush, his life was in big trouble. The sound of the metal blades on that mower crunchin' limbs and glass light bulbs was something awful. Mrs. Sullivan ran out of her door in her favorite Mickey Mouse robe and threw herself to the ground in front of the chopped up mess.

Although I felt real sorry for Tim right at that moment, I also felt real sure he wasn't the one for me. If I had started seein' him, I knew Mrs. Sullivan would stop seeing me. We weren't real good friends or anything, but she made the best tuna noodle casserole you ever did want to eat. Every time she makes one, she brings a big plate over to me. I didn't think Tim was worth those tuna casseroles.

The second boy Jesus sent for me to consider was Spencer Yarborough. He worked at the bank during the week and taught Sunday school at the church. We usually never said too much to each other. Just a "Blessed morning to you, brother" or a "May God bless you, sister" here and there. But the week after I asked God to send me a partner, Spencer seemed to see me in a whole different light.

On Monday mornings, the church's quiltin' group gets together. They were working on making Reverend Sanders a quilt for his upcoming birthday. Usually, it's a pretty small group, but they were strugglin' to finish the quilt on time. They asked for anyone who had any experience quiltin' or sewing to please make an effort to be at the fellowship hall that week. I told Mandy, the leader of the quiltin' group, I hadn't ever quilted before, but I would help if she needed me. Without hidin' it at all, she looked down her nose at me. Those quiltin' ladies can be kind of snooty, like their quilts are the most important thing in creation. But for Reverent Sanders, I was willin' to put up with their uppity ways for a morning. Mandy told me she supposed they could find something for me to do. I got to the fellowship hall that morning, and Mandy handed me a pair of scissors and a stack of fabric.

"Come on with me," she commanded. "We're going to let you cut out the quilt pieces and use this iron-on tacking to stick them together. Then we'll be able to stitch and quilt them. It's real important that you cut along the pattern carefully, otherwise, the pieces won't match up and the squares will be ruined. If that happens, we'll be giving Reverend Sanders a pillow, instead of the beautiful quilt we've started. After you get the pieces cut out, you'll need to follow the pattern and iron them together."

She nodded over to a long table that held the quilt squares that had already been sewn together. They were laid out like a picture book. There was Adam and Eve on the top, with flowers growing in front of their private parts. Next came Cain and Able. Cain was hoverin' over Able with a rock in his hand and looking all kind of angry. I got real excited to be a part of such a pretty thing.

"What Bible story am I going to be working on?" I asked Mandy.

"Jonah and the whale."

I took my scissors and my fabric and headed to a table to begin. I had to remind myself that morning that we are all created equal. I didn't really feel equal to Mandy and her crowd. Their hair was perfectly poofed, and they sipped coffee from Styrofoam cups while chatting about all kinds of stuff. I wanted to make a good impression, 'cause I didn't usually get a chance to be a part of this particular group. So I jumped into my chore, being nothin' but careful and particular. I didn't want to be the reason Jonah and the whale wasn't displayed on Reverend Sander's bed.

After about an hour or so, I was feelin' much more comfortable. I had cut out all my pieces and was almost done ironing them together. I decided to pour myself a cup of coffee, so I could sip it like the rest of the girls. They looked so fancy. I don't drink coffee. I much prefer a Mountain Dew, if I need a little pick-me-up. But I was real determined to sit and have a cup like Mandy and the quiltin' group. As they chatted about how tacky the dress was that Sue Lewis wore to church on Sunday, I took a sip of that thick black coffee. I know that the Lord was lookin' after me in that moment, because I normally would have spit that nasty stuff straight across the floor. Instead, I managed to keep all but a few drops in my mouth. The drops that didn't stay in, dripped right down onto Jonah's face. Now, he looked like a colored Jonah. I gasped and unfortunately, Mandy heard me.

"Is something wrong?" she quickly asked.

I grabbed the quilt square and held it to my chest. I know I should have been honest in that moment, but I didn't want to embarrass myself in front of the quiltin' ladies.

"No, no. I just swallowed wrong. That's all."

Mandy stared at me for a few moments. I just smiled at her and pretended to take another sip of coffee. After she got back to work, I looked down at Jonah's dark brown face. "Oh, shit!" was really all I could think of, although I knew it was a sin to even think a cuss word in church. I remembered seein' a colored Jesus once in a picture book. "Maybe Jonah was black," I thought. I tried real hard to convince myself I could make the black face work. But the more I worried about what I was going to say to Mandy, the more I knew I was going to have to fix this. And I was goin' to have to fix it without her noticin' that anything was wrong.

I couldn't let Mandy see I was cutting something from the square. So I studied it for a minute — real careful. I put my scissors right over Jonah's forehead, and held the square cloth close to my chest. As cautiously as I could, while lookin' out the window so as not to arouse suspicion, I cut the little circle face from the quilt square. She never knew what happened.

I picked up the scraps from the peach fabric that I had cut Jonah's face from in the first place, and I cut another little face and ironed it right where it was supposed to be. After another hour, I was done with Jonah's square and, as I told myself then, done quiltin'. I proudly walked up to Mandy and handed her my square. She looked at it, and then looked back at me with a look of shock, followed by a big ol' smile. I was guessin' she didn't think I could do as good as I'd done.

I headed from the church over to the bank to deposit my weekly check from PayPal. As I walked over to the counter, Spencer, who was the teller, turned and looked over at me. That's when I noticed it. He is usually all business and polite and all. This morning, he was stumblin' over his words and lookin' all nervous and such. I've seen what love-struck looks like in movies. You blush, you can't say what you're tryin' to say, you're embarrassed to look someone you fancy in the eyes. He had all the symptoms. And at that moment, I knew he was bachelor number two. I remember thinkin' he was a nice enough guy and all, but he just always gave me the heebie-jeebies. I had to ask Jesus to forgive me for this, since Spencer is one of His children, and he is a real good Sunday school teacher.

Actually, Spencer was so nervous that day, he made my deposit in record time. I thought he was trying to impress me by how good he did his job. It wadn't until I got home, went to the bathroom, and looked in the mirror that I realized why he was workin' so hard to get my deposit finished.

I nearly fell over flat when I noticed there was a little hole cut right out of my tank top. That little circle was just the size of Jonah's head and just the size of my nipple, which was peerin' right out at me!

I thanked Jesus for tending to my prayer request so quickly, but I asked if maybe he could go about it in a little less embarrassing way in the future. I now use the PayPal direct deposit feature to get my money into my bank account.

Wayne Darell stumbled into my life just three days later. I'm happy to say that when I met him, all my private parts were completely tucked away.

Wayne is a handyman of sorts. He does odd jobs here and there around town. He likes to have the freedom to work when he wants to. No regular nine to five job for him. He's a free spirit who just moved to town a few months ago.

I was at the church helpin' Reverend Sanders clean out the children's nursery school room the week after the quiltin' mess. If he had asked for me to help him on the same day Mandy and her quiltin' friends was gonna' be there, I would have had to turn him down. But, he needed some assistance on Wednesday, so I was in the clear.

Reverend Sanders asked me to start sorting through some arts and crafts stuff in this big ol' cabinet. The whole thing smelled like Play Dough and Elmer's glue. There must have been a million little scraps of construction paper piled in the bottom of it. I set to scoopin' them into a dust pan, when a big old roach jumped out onto my hand. I'm not talkin' about one of those little ones. I'm talkin' about a roach so big, it could cover my hand. There's just something about those dirty bugs that sets my skin to crawlin'. So when he jumped on my hand, I screamed like a big old baby. Then I jumped up and threw all the paper bits I'd collected straight up into the air. It was the town's Fourth of July parade happenin' inside the Sunday school room!

Suddenly, a big strong hand grabbed my shoulder. As I looked back, I saw Wayne Darell comin' into the room in a tight white tee-shirt, smiling at me, as bits of color paper rained down around us. It was like something straight out of a movie! Things were movin' in slow-motion. All I could think of was God's promise to Noah with his rainbow. As the colored paper floated around Wayne Darell's handsome face, I thought, "He must be God's promise to me."

Most folks, I think, don't get those movie kind of moments often, so I decided to take full advantage of it. I knew exactly what would come next in a movie. So I jumped into his arms, looked at him with sexy eyes, and kissed him right on the mouth. Let me just say right now I am not "that kind" of girl. I would never kiss a boy I've never even said more than hello to; but since God was orchestratin' this whole thing, I wanted to make it special. The only problem was, when I locked my lips on his and started the most passionate kiss I was ever gonna' have in my life, the one we would tell our children about, I tasted something awful. Before I knew it, there was a big old wad of chew in my mouth and drippin' down my chin. Wayne Darell was lookin' at me like I was crazy. Then, in walked Reverend Sanders. He took in the mess around the room and the mess all over my chin and put his hand to his chest.

Wayne set me back onto the floor and grabbed the small trash can in the corner and spit the rest of that nasty stuff in there, while wiping his mouth on that tee-shirt that was so white a few moments before. I took one look at the chew that *was fallin' from his lips and immediately threw up in the plastic box of crayons sitting on the table.*

I told Reverend Sanders I would come back to finish up after lunch. I had to get home to my toothbrush. Wayne stayed to finish paintin' the choir room. I was beginnin' to wonder if I had misread God's signs. Maybe Wayne wasn't the fella' God had intended for me. But after I went home and got all cleaned up, I went back to the church. Wayne was standing in the hallway watching for me.

"Hey, darlin'. What say we try that kiss again later tonight?"

I knew right then the signs had been crystal clear. How could I have doubted our construction paper scraps rainbow?

6 Arnold at the Shop and Save

Arnold had been a gangly kid growing up, with bad eyesight. As if skinny legs and thick glasses weren't enough, he also had terrible acne as a teen. He wasn't athletic and didn't play sports. Now, some might think that, although the odds were against him, he must have been smart . . . or maybe a musical prodigy. Perhaps a spelling bee champion or the president of the chess club? None of that was true, either. Arnold was your average "Joe Schmo," all the way around.

During his senior year in high school, two things became clear to him—he might never have a date, and he *would* have to attend the junior college. No girl would give him a second glance, and his grades weren't good enough to get him into a four-year college. When he graduated, Arnold enrolled at Florida Community College. And though he didn't have much of a clue about what he wanted to "become," he studied hard during his two years there, taking mostly general education classes. It helped that there weren't the usual distractions many college students faced. Girls avoided him, and he was overlooked when invites were given out to keg parties.

After finishing junior college, Arnold applied for a job at the local Shop and Save. In a "moment of clarity," he'd decided working was going to get him further than college. He started as a bagger and quickly moved up to being a cashier. Since he didn't cause any problems, rarely made mistakes and didn't take cigarette breaks every thirty minutes, as most of the employees did, Arnold slowly, but surely moved through the Shop and Save ranks. After five years, he was made store manager.

Luck had come his way when Chuck, the previous manager, was blamed for stealing filet mignons and wine. It seems he would wander about the store watching for pretty women who didn't wear a wedding ring. When he'd spot one, he would grab a bottle of merlot and two filet mignons, just as his prey was about to check out. He'd bag the wine and steaks, tuck them in his brief case, and tell the cashiers he was clocking out. Then he'd hop into his car and follow her home. As she'd begin getting the grocery bags from her car, he would hurriedly park, remove the Shop and Save bag from his briefcase, and run up the sidewalk.

"Excuse me, ma'am?" he would begin. "I believe you left this bag at the register. I'm the manager of the store, Chuck. I called out to you in the parking lot, but you didn't hear me. So, I followed you all the way here to bring it to you. Customer service is our priority, you know."

Any of the women he'd target would look at Chuck with appreciation.

"Oh, goodness! You followed me all the way *here*? I can't believe it! Here, let me take that bag from you."

She would open it and realize it wasn't her bag.

"I'm so sorry to tell you this, but this isn't my bag. Bless your heart, though! You came all the way here for nothing."

He would feign a look of surprise.

"Oh, it's okay, ma'am. I was just heading home, anyway. I'll never be able to figure out who this belongs to. I guess I'll return it to the store tomorrow, in case someone comes to ask for it." He would shake his head, as if confused. "Maybe I'll just have steak and wine for dinner, and sort all of this out tomorrow."

Chuck was a nice looking man. Not what you would call "handsome," but cute, in a boyish looking way . . . even though he *was* thirty years old. He tried his best to look corporate in his Shop and Save name badge. And with his blond hair cut short, playful blue eyes and a tan during the summer months, if he flashed a smile at one of the unsuspecting women, he knew they were putty in his hands.

Chuck would pause a moment, smile, and then say, "Y'know, I'll have a hard time eating all this steak by myself. If you don't mind me asking, are you single? I don't suppose you'd like to share a steak dinner and a bottle of wine?"

Something about seeing Chuck at the Shop and Save every week made him seem like an old friend. Not someone who could possibly be a serial killer or a stalker. The ladies' typical reaction would be, *What harm could come from having dinner with this nice manager from my grocery store?* A few glasses of wine later, they'd find out there was no harm at all. In fact, as far as their libido was concerned, it actually did them a world of good!

Chuck knew how to inventory products, demand quality control in the produce department, schedule employees and drive a woman to the brink of ecstasy — or so many of the the single ladies around town said. He always made the woman he was with feel amazing.

Chuck was enjoying the perks of his job, and the Shop and Save was always busy. Things were swell, until the corporate department came for a surprise visit. The missing steaks and wine were noted. Security footage was reviewed and Chuck was immediately out of a job . . . *and* out of the Shop and Save's single female clients.

As corporate probed into Chuck's escapades, they decided the new manager would need to be straight as an arrow, and preferably not good-looking or charming. Since Arnold was in all things opposite of Chuck, he was the perfect replacement. Arnold was often in awe of the way the customers seemed to react to Chuck. They spoke to him as if they were old friends. He wondered how he would ever be able to pull off handling his new position. He had worked at the store for five years, but only a handful of customers seemed to know his name. Still, while he worried about taking the job, the extra cash sounded good, especially since he was still living in his parent's garage apartment.

Things went slowly for a while. Every other customer who walked into the store asked Arnold where Chuck was. Corporate had instructed him about how to answer such questions. His response was to be, "He decided to make a career change. Shop and Save will miss him, but we support our employees as they move onto other endeavors."

Arnold regurgitated the quote so often, he heard it in his sleep. It took about four months for the questions to begin to wane. Then, he only had to occasionally explain Chuck's absence. At the time of Chuck's firing, corporate didn't enlighten Arnold as to the reason for his departure. However, Chuck was fine about letting Arnold in on his secret, and one day told him.

"I had the time of my life here at Shop and Save, man. I got more ass than I could have gotten in a sorority house. It's all about the ladies. Find a way to charm the ladies, and you'll have this job in the palm of your hand," he confided.

Looking at Chuck's handsome smile, Arnold realized the pursuit of bringing the female customers swooning to their knees would never work for him. He saw himself every day in the mirror. However, he never forgot Chuck's advice. Mustering up what masculinity he could, he tried to speak to all the lady customers and give the ladies compliments. It just didn't come very naturally. But one day, something happened to change his life.

It started as he was checking the mister over the produce case. As he bent his head under to see that all was in place, the mister came on, spraying water all over his face. Since water drops had splashed his glasses, he straightened up, the whole produce section looked smeared and blurred. That's when he saw, or actually heard, Eve Plowers talking to Judy Nuberg.

"If only they sold Gucci at Shop and Save! I can get away with a $200 grocery bill, but a $200 bill at Macy's would throw Charles into a tailspin," complained Eve.

"I know what you mean. I paid for one dress five different ways the other day at Betsy Johnson. I damn near used every credit card in my wallet, along with the $32.76 I was going to use for lunch with a girlfriend. Todd would have killed me if he had known I spent $324.00 on one dress," replied Judy.

Eve laughed and shook her head. "Stay out of trouble, now." She raised her hand to wave goodbye to Judy. The Coach purse that was slung over her wrist as she waved hung briefly in the air. As Arnold tried to adjust his vision with the water running down his glasses, he saw Eve's glamorous purse shimmer in front of the door leading to the back storeroom. It was like a sign.

Arnold immediately clocked out for lunch and barricaded himself in his office. He had managed to save quite a nest egg while living with his parents. Although it wasn't enough to get his own place, it was enough to carry out his plan. Within three days, he had set up a corporation which sold women's clothing and accessories. *Doughmaker225* from the *Start Your Own Boutique* chat room was kind enough to share some of her resources. A large, regional vendor's market was coming up in six weeks. Arnold scheduled three vacation days and booked a flight to Atlanta.

He began noticing every bag, blouse and pair of shoes that walked into his store. He also began complimenting the women on their outfits. Sometimes, he would ask questions like, "That handbag is so nice. I would love to get one for my girlfriend. Her birthday is in July. Do you mind me asking where you bought it?"

Arnold spent hours thumbing through magazines on the store's magazine rack. *Cosmopolitan* and *InStyle* were his gold mines. Before long, his plan was ready for launching. He had put a new lock on one of the vacant offices off of the storeroom, and was the only one with a key, except Vaughn, the store bookkeeper. She was indispensable to his plan. It was her idea to name their business "Shop or Save." Since it was so close to "Shop and Save," if a husband or boyfriend saw the name on a check or a credit card statement, they wouldn't think twice. Vaughn promised Arnold there was no way corporate would ever get wind of their plan. She would keep the books and take care of the taxes.

Until he could gauge the success of his venture, Arnold didn't want to let any of the other employees in on it. Of course, if they *did* hear about it, somehow, he was sure providing them witha few seasonal accessories could urge them to keep their mouths shut.

Since he considered Eve the spark that ignited his plan, he decided to start with her. He waited for three days until she finally came into the store. Walking up behind her, he tapped her on the shoulder as she was comparing the ingredients in the Fruit Loops and the Frosted Flakes.

"Excuse me, Mrs. Plowers?"

Eve turned and looked at Arnold. He noticed her Minolo Blanak shoes and her Gucci watch, and knew he had waited for the perfect shopper.

"I was wondering if I could have a quick word with you."

Eve looked perplexed, but didn't want to seem rude. "Sure, um- . . ." She glanced at his name tag. ". . . Arnold."

They never had to look at Chuck's nametag, he thought. But that was all going to change. Arnold could feel it.

"I just received some new merchandise I think you might be very interested in. Being one of our most stylish customers, I was hoping you could take a look. It'll only take a minute."

Eve followed Arnold to the back room. She had her hand in her purse and was clutching her pepper spray, just in case "Mr. Coke Bottle Glasses" thought he might try something funny. Arnold opened the door to the room and, *immediately,* Eve squealed in delight.

"Is that the new Coach purse? It's backordered online!" She walked to the back wall and grabbed a cashmere sweater and ruffled the soft fabric. Spinning around, Eve stared at a pair of Kate Spade sunglasses, which had just been on the cover of *InStyle*.

She looked at Arnold with her eyebrow raised. "What exactly is this room?"

Arnold explained to her that his brainchild had been born after listening to her conversation with her friend months ago. "I decided I had it in my power to help you ladies out. I plan on stocking the most current fashion-forward (he had learned that word by watching the Style Channel) clothing and accessories. I'll open the store to ladies around town. They can purchase anything they like. The beauty is, my corporation is named 'Shop or Save.' That is, of course, who you'll make your check out to and the name that will appear on your credit card bills."

A light switched on in Eve's head. Her face lit up and she began jumping up and down, clapping her hands. "That is brilliant! Absolutely brilliant! Al will never know whether I bought a new purse or snacks for my son's soccer team. I could hide a new necklace inside the food for a dinner party!" She ran across the room and hugged Arnold.

A smile spread across his face. He had finally found a way to make his mark, to stand up and be noticed.

"Now, Eve," he said. "The only way this will work is if it is kept totally quiet. I will let you have first pick of every new shipment I receive, *if* you'll help me spread the word to people you know and trust."

"Not only will I let everyone know, I'll also kill anyone who breathes a word about it to anyone who can't be trusted."

Eve left the back storeroom holding the cashmere sweater, compliments of Shop or Save. She decided on a secret phrase that would let Arnold know if one of the store's customers was safe to admit.

"I'm looking for guava jelly and persimmons," was the glorious phrase that would admit someone into the Shop or Save's boutique. Other employees soon began to catch on; and as planned, Arnold let them occasionally take merchandise as a "thank you" for their cooperation. Many of the Shop and Save employees would *never* have been able to sport Prada sunglasses or wear silk scarves, if it hadn't been for Shop or Save. All in all, everyone was happy. The shoppers, the employees, Vaughn, and most of all, Arnold.

That was just the problem. Arnold, although he had never suffered depression, had also never been truly happy. Once he began to feel it, it just didn't feel right. Nothing had ever been easy for him. Nothing had ever gone right for him. Nobody had ever known his name or looked at him with an appreciative (let alone affectionate) smile. A foreboding came over him every time he deposited another check into the Shop or Save account, which by now was upwards of $15,000 (for just a few month's work).

He spent his nights worrying about what might happen—trying to see into the future and wondering how to avoid disaster. Since, as far as he could tell, his bases were covered, Arnold couldn't foresee anything bad happening. He felt he was in control. *But*, he thought, *a little extra insurance couldn't hurt*. He hit the Payment button on his Paypal account and deposited $49.00 into "the prayer lady's" account.

7 KEEPIN' YOUR PRAYERS IN YOUR CLOSET

*Our heavenly Father, please forgive my sins.
I'm calling on you now for your daughter, Frankie.
This may not sound as strange to you as it does to
me, but my job is only to bring the prayer to you.
So I won't question it. Dear Lord, Frankie is
asking that you give her parties. Parties like those
she used to throw. Parties with lots of people,
dancin', good conversations, and a little bit of
trouble — hopefully nothing that you wouldn't
approve of. Dear Lord, please bring parties back
into Frankie's life. In the name of your precious
Son. Amen.*

Every once in a while, I get strange requests like
Frankie's. I'm just wonderin' what is going on in some
peoples' minds. I mean, who prays for parties? It seems
pretty weird, but it ain't the weirdest request I ever got. One
time, this guy asked me to pray that the good Lord give

him – and I'm quotin' him, now – "the ability to figure out the quantum physics to design a time machine to transport me back to the year 1982." Now, how do you even go about that? It's right tricky to pray for somethin', if you don't even know what it is. I'm guessing it wadn't a literal time machine the guy wanted. He was just wantin' to go back to a time in his life that was good, so he could remember God's blessings. Or maybe he messed something up real bad and wanted to fix it. He paid me for a whole year. One hundred and forty dollars was deposited into my PayPal account at the beginning of each month like clockwork. That was $1,820.00 for the whole year!

I guess we all wish we could go back to some time in our lives and change somethin' or other. I would definitely change my morning with the quiltin' ladies. But I wouldn't change a minute of my time with Wayne.

He took me out on a date after that day in the Sunday school room. We went to Lucky's Bar to dance. Turned out that Wayne was as good a dancer as he was a handyman. He was a perfect gentleman that first night. Got me home by 11:30 and offered to go to church with me on Sunday morning. That surprised me a little bit, seein' as how the only time I had seen Wayne at church was when he was fixin' something.

After our first date, I thought Wayne was as heavenly as Mrs. Sullivan's twinkle light rose bush before the accident. So, when he didn't show up for church like he'd said he would, I didn't get mad; I was just a little disappointed. I had worn the flowered sundress I bought for my cousin's wedding a few years before. I only wore it on special occasions. He told me later he got called out to fix a pipe over at the diner. If anyone knows about a job taking up almost every minute of your day, it's me. So what could I really say?

I was jumpin' into a new chapter in my life. I ain't never had a boyfriend — at least not since high school — so I had some catchin' up to do, as far as gettin' familiar with havin' Wayne around. Pretty quick, he began coming over most days after work. We'd eat supper together and watch TV. He mostly watched ballgames, which was fine with me, because I'd use that time to catch up on my emails and stuff. Every once in a while, I would even say some of my prayers during this time. I'd just kind of tune out the clapping and cheering on the TV and talk to God quietly in my own head. I had a few more clients, so every minute was important. I couldn't let anyone's prayers be forgotten.

For a long time, after we started seein' each other, Wayne didn't know about my prayer business. That was something I just didn't tell people. I always think back to Matthew 6:6 — "But thou, when thou prayest, enter into thy closet, and when thou hast shut thy door, pray to thy Father which is in secret; and thy Father which seeth in secret shall reward thee openly."

I don't know whether or not I would have ever told Wayne about my prayer business, but he walked by my computer one day, when I had left an email open. I was going to the bathroom and didn't think he'd be comin' over until later. He hollered hello as he walked in, grabbed a beer and sat on the sofa, right where my computer was sittin'. The fact there was a receipt from PayPal for "Prayer Services Rendered" in the amount of $140.00 sure caught his eye. When I walked out of the back of the trailer, he was sittin' there with a big ol' smile on his face.

"What's this, babe?" he asked, as he nodded toward the computer. "That ain't your money, is it?"

I took a deep breath and thought about what to say next. Two things made me tell him about my business. One was, I just don't like lyin'. I try to take the Ten Commandments very serious. Next was, I thought, since God sent Wayne to me, maybe he was the one for me. That meant we'd probably get married one day. Everyone knows that husbands and wives are supposed to give theirselves to each other completely. So I figured I'd just go ahead and get a head start on that.

I thought Wayne might laugh at me when I told him, but he didn't laugh at all. He nodded his head and smiled, as I told him about all my clients. When I finished, he reached his arm around me and pulled me into his lap. I near cried when he looked me in the eyes and said for the first time, "I love you, darlin'."

I kinda looked up at Wayne to make sure he wasn't smirking or nothing. I wadn't sure how anyone else would take my prayer business. I couldn't see a trace of anything bad in his eyes. He asked about my clients and what kind of things they asked me to pray for. Then he asked how much I made each month from my prayin'. I figured I'd save that until there wadn't nothin' else to save. I wadn't ready to lose my virginity or my bank account balance right at that time. So, I just told him I made enough to take care of myself and put a little money away for a rainy day. He didn't ask no more questions, right then. Just gave me a kiss and turned on a baseball game.

I didn't think much more about it, until a few days later. Wayne came home from the church, where he'd been doin' some yardwork for Reverend Sanders. His intention had been just to plant a few azaleas next to the handicap ramp going up into the sanctuary. The cold got to the old ones, and they was nothing but sticks. As he was pullin' the dead ones up, though, he found some dry rot on the side of the handicap ramp. He pulled off a few pieces of the wood and showed Reverend Sanders the damage. The Reverend gave him a check for materials and his time, and sent him off to the hardware store for supplies. Before he left, Wayne went ahead and pulled off most the side of that ramp to get a head start before headin' to the store.

While he was at the store, old Mrs. Whipple came rollin' up to the church in her electric scooter. She was comin' by to check on the candles in the sanctuary. She always made sure they never melted too low — she did a real fine job, too. Well, when she started up that ramp, she began to feel the ramp shake a little and start to lean to the side, due to the fact the thing was near about torn apart. She tried to put her electric scooter into reverse, but the pedal malfunctioned and got jammed. Instead of backing up, that scooter jerked forward with such force the whole ramp just collapsed. Poor Mrs. Whipple got stuck under it, and she broke her hip, her rib, and her leg.

Wayne pulled up in his truck, all loaded with lumber and whatnot, and heard Mrs. Whipple repeatin', "The Lord is my shepherd, I shall not want." He told me later he was shakin' like a leaf when he pulled the wood off her leg and drove her down to the hospital.

After all the commotion died down, he came over and asked me if I would mind sayin' a prayer for Mrs. Whipple. He seemed right shook up and a bit scared, too. Mrs. Whipple's son was some hotshot attorney in the city, and she was always blabbing around town about what havoc her son could wreak when there was an injustice. Well, when he heard about what happened with the scooter he'd bought his mamma for her birthday, he was madder than an old wet hen. Luckily for Wayne, Mrs. Whipple's son threw his anger at the scooter company and not at Wayne for being careless. He threatened to take that scooter company to the cleaners for that faulty pedal. They must've got scared . . . 'cuz by the time Mrs. Whipple came home from the hospital a few days later and started reading through all her mail that had been pilin' up, she got a letter from the company.

They apologized for the malfunction of the reverse pedal, and told her she would be receiving the latest model of their scooter in a few days. The letter went on to say they had already contacted the hospital, and they would be taking care of all her hospital bills. There was also a check for any mental anguish. They must have thought she anguished quite a bit, because the check was in the amount of $15,000.

The next Sunday, Mrs. Whipple was back at church with her leg and arm in casts. She came right up the ramp Wayne had fixed, sittin' on her brand new scooter. The elementary Sunday school class had made a banner for her scooter that was taped across the back seat. It read,

"The Lord is near to the brokenhearted and saves those who are crushed in spirit" (and by ramps). Psalm 34:18

There were flowers and crosses painted around the verse. You could tell they worked real hard on it. I'm guessing they used the supplies I had organized in the art cabinet just a few weeks before. There wadn't much room for Mrs. Whipple's new scooter in the sanctuary. It looked almost double the size of her old one and was painted a bright red. Yep, it was a real fancy model with rearview mirrors and big ol' wheels.

As she tried to make her way up the middle aisle, I saw that that wadn't gonna' work. Since I was passing out bulletins that day, I figured I should probably help her find a place to park her scooter. I managed to get her right up next to the organ. It was kinda' loud with the organ blaring right there, but that was the only place in the sanctuary with enough room. Funny, it was where we usually put the Christmas tree. Since we were in August, at the time, I knew she'd be set for a while, anyway.

As I helped her put on the parking brake, she grabbed my arm and leaned in to me. "You got yourself a right good man in Wayne," she said, as Mrs. Lessing, the organist, played right next to us.

I smiled and nodded in agreement. She motioned with her finger for me to lean in close to her face. She smelled like moth balls and the rose perfume Mammaw used to wear. "He told me about the prayer lady he paid to pray for me after my tragedy. He told me he was sure her prayers were the reason I didn't have any permanent damage and that the insurance company was so quick to cooperate with my son. He's a good man for finding a woman with such faith."

I sucked in my breath and shot straight up. As the organ music got louder and louder, I got more and more mad. How could he tell someone my secret? I had made him promise not to tell a soul.

Mrs. Whipple winked at me and held up her finger. As she opened her mouth to speak, I saw from the corner of my eye that Mrs. Lessing had lifted her fingers from the keys in the grand way she always does at the end of a song. The organ stopped in just the moment that Mrs. Whipple said way too loud, "Just watch him on the internet, dear. Everyone loves to put their sex on there."

Mrs. Whipple just smiled and nodded. She didn't even notice the rest of the churchgoers around her were gasping in shock. And though I wanted to dive under the pews, I let out a big breath of relief! He had told Mrs. Whipple about his prayer lady — he just didn't tell her it was me. "The prayer lady" was just somebody on the internet to Mrs. Whipple. He had kept my secret.

At the end of the service, Reverend Sanders thanked Mrs. Whipple for donating $500 to the candle fund. With such a big donation, her previous outburst was quickly forgotten.

When I got home that night and checked on my accounts, I found a payment from PayPal in the amount of $1,500. The payment was accompanied by a note that said, "Thank you *for the prayers you prayed for me on Wayne Darell's request. Your friend in the Lord, Mrs. Wilhelmina Whipple."*

8 FRANKIE'S PARTY

Frankie stood in her kitchen and stared at the hibiscuses blooming by her pool. She smiled, noticing the bush was full of blooms, the way they were when she and Ed had moved into the house. Her eyes watered thinking about it, though. Life had become so lonely for her, since Ed had passed twelve years ago to the day. A heart attack had stolen the only heart Frankie had ever really loved. Not that Ed was the *only* man she was ever with. No, Frankie had certainly made the rounds in her younger days.

The fact is, Frankie had always had the charisma and flair of a flapper from the 20's . . . always eccentric and on the lookout for fun. However, she was also a "disco queen," and perfectly at ease with nudity and the occasional line of cocaine. Indeed, "partying" seemed to have been part of her genetic makeup.

The things that shape a person's life and

attitude can be quite telling. Francis, Frankie's mother, was a stickler for order and perfect behavior. She kept a house without so much as a thing out of place and a daughter without so much as a hair out of place. Frankie was to have a clean room, ironed clothes, and perfect grades . . . *always*. There wasn't time for much else.

"Young ladies don't need to be wandering around town," Francis would tell Frankie on a daily basis, whenever she asked to go out to get a malt with her friends.

The one place Frankie could escape to without her mother's criticism was her grandmother's house. Grams lived next door. In Frankie's mind, her home was the best place in the world to be. She would walk next door and marvel at the fact her mother was Grams's offspring.

Grams seemed stuck in the 1920's. She introduced Frankie to the flapper's lifestyle. Frankie always considered Grams to be exciting and eccentric. As she got older, however, she wondered if Grams was a bit senile. Grams just couldn't leave behind the memories of her carefree, wild times, where rules were ignored and independence was gold. It didn't matter, though. There wasn't a time when she walked into Grams's house that her Victrola wasn't playing "Happy Feet" or "I Wanna' Be Loved by You."

Frankie's mother definitely thought Grams was losing it. She watched after her the way someone watches after a plant that needs to be occasionally watered and pruned. With her mother's help, Grams's mortgage was paid each month, her groceries were purchased, and she was treated to a weekly trip to the hair salon. Other than those basic necessities, Francis didn't have time for Grams's foolishness and craziness. She often contemplated putting her into a home, whenever she seemed to lose sight of reality. However, at this point, Grams didn't pose a threat to herself; so she decided to let things lie, until she couldn't take it anymore.

Frankie, however, adored Grams. It was always the same, every time she walked into Grams's house.

"Are you on the lam again? My daughter can be such a wet blanket, can't she, doll? You just come on in here."

So Frankie did. She would sit and listen to the jazz music playing away, while Grams sipped on her "hooch" and told her about the wild parties she used to go to, which were always filled with bootleg liquor and the good-looking men they referred to as sheiks. Grams described it all in such detail, that Frankie could almost see it in her mind's eye. Grams even went so far as to teach Frankie the Charleston.

"Look at those gams move!" she would exclaim, as she watched Frankie effortlessly kick her feet back and forth.

Frankie spent many an afternoon in Grams' "fun home." When Frankie reached driving age, her mother gladly turned over the beauty shop trips to Frankie. Francis hated sitting in the perm-smelling salon, full of old women chatting about cleaning products or recipes. She was sure she had the upper hand on any of this information. These women had *nothing* she cared to hear. Interestingly, Grams eventually saw this was the way many of the caretakers felt about the weekly trips to the beauty shop. She watched as nurses, daughters, and sometimes even grown sons rolled their eyes and checked their watches, over and over again, agitated at wasting time in a salon. That's when the idea hit her.

"Frankie, we need a jitney to take all us old dames to the parlor. You could drive us, Ducky! Wouldn't that just be the cat's meow!"

"Sounds fine , but I don't have a car."

"Oh, applesauce! I've got a perfectly good 1961 Thunderbird in the shed out back."

"Grandpop's car?"

"Yes. He'd be keen on us putting some miles on that jalopy. The old hayburner is just taking up space. I don't think Grandpop is going to be needing it anytime soon. What do you say?"

"Well, I don't know. My mom probably won't allow it."

"Mrs. Grundy doesn't have to know. I'll tell all the gals not to spill the beans! I'm sure they'd be happy to turn over some moolah to you in return."

"Well, I guess I could drive you and a few friends," Frankie replied.

Frankie became affectionately known as "the savior of the blue hairs." However, driving Grams' elderly lady-friends to the salon turned into a bit more than Frankie imagined. She became the driver, the provider of liquor, the supplier of smokes, and, to her delight, the face of fun.

At first, it was all pretty tame. She would schedule a pickup time with the nurse, daughter, daughter-in-law, or sometimes the ladies themselves. She would shuttle them to the beauty salon, and then take them home an hour or two later. She had enjoyed Grams's company for so long, it never occurred to her the women getting their gray hair permed or curled in rollers might not be anything but entertaining. She loved sitting on the vinyl sofa with a soda, as she listened to the tales from their younger days.

Darcy Lovely was one of Grams's best friends. She couldn't have been more than five feet tall, but that five feet was all she needed. She had actually made children walking past her drop their ice-cream cones and run in fear — with just a look! It was known among most people in town, Frankie came to find out, to cross Mrs. Lovely was like crossing a black bear that was past his hibernation time. Frankie had been quite nervous about picking her up for the first time. She asked Grams if she would ride with her, which she was happy to do, if it meant getting out of the house and spending time with friends.

Darcy lived at the Twilight Time assisted living facility. As the Thunderbird pulled up into the circular drive, Darcy came barreling out of the front door, waving her hands in the air, while a wispy looking nurse ran after her holding out a cup.

"Please, Mrs. Lovely, you need to take your vitamins. They'll make you feel so good. And your hair will be so nice and shiny and soft."

"Those damn vitamins stop me up like a cork! And if you think I give a damn about how my hair feels, you're even more dumb than I thought! Other than my beautician, *nobody* has touched my hair since my husband died fifteen years ago! You can shove that cup of vitamins up your ass, then you'll see how constipated I feel!"

Frankie watched open-mouthed, as Mrs. Lovely got into the car and slammed the door with what looked like every last ounce of strength was left in that eighty-seven-year-old body.

"Close your mouth, dear, or you'll catch a fly," she quipped at Frankie.

Frankie nodded and pulled out of the drive.

"Is that twit gumming up the works again?" Grams asked.

"She's always hovering over me, like I'm going to keel over any minute! Thank God I get to escape Twilight once a week."

As they arrived at the salon, Frankie debated on whether or not to help Mrs. Lovely out of the car. She felt like she should at least open the car door for her. But after the rant they had listened to on the way over, she decided she would escape Lovely's wrath more readily if she left her to her own devices. Frankie glanced over her shoulder, as she opened the salon door to see Mrs. Lovely promenading up the sidewalk with Grams at her side, laughing as if they were teenagers. As they walked through the door, Mrs. Lovely winked at Frankie.

"You might just be okay," she said.

Frankie smiled, knowing she had just passed the test. What she *didn't* know was how many more tests she was going to have to pass with this group of gray-haired trouble makers.

Once the ladies were inside, Frankie left the salon, since she had two more ladies — both who lived on Alta Road — to deliver to the salon. After that, her last run would be to the east side of town. There were three ladies there. Upon hearing that Frankie would be running carpool for Grams's friends, Grams asked Suzi at the salon if she could reserve one afternoon just for this particular group.

"We'll tip you really well, if we can have the salon all to ourselves," Grams said. "It'll also be good if my dear friend Mrs. Lovely isn't around your other paying clients. She is getting more and more ornery every day."

Suzi knew that Grams had a valid point, so she declared Tuesday afternoons booked until further notice. Frankie's "clients" declared it the Gray Haired Speakeasy, which was Grams's idea.

On the first day of their appointments, Mrs. Lovely pulled the shades to the windows that overlooked Main Street.

"Oh, Mrs. Lovely, the light is so bad in here. I do really prefer to work with the shades open," Suzi remarked.

With that, Mrs. Lovely pulled out a bottle of whisky, opened the lid and took a giant swig without so much as a grimace. She held the bottle out to Suzi and said, "Lighten up, young lady. How old are you?"

"Twenty-seven."

"Twenty-seven? There's still hope. You don't want to end up like my uptight daughter-in-law do you? Take a few shots of this, and you won't care if you cut my hair blindfolded!"

"Oh, wouldn't that just be a hoot!" Grams laughed. "We'll have to remember that for one of our future soirees!"

With that, Suzi took a sip from the bottle.

"*Music*," Grams said. "*That's* what we need. Grab my purse for me, will ya, doll?" she asked Frankie.

Grams pulled out a record and handed it to Frankie, while nodding to the record player in the corner of the room.

Suzi smiled. "I haven't played music in here since Mrs. Pearl claimed the racket from the radio distracted me and ruined her hair! She said I cut a bald patch right up front. Truth is, she's losing her hair faster than my balding mailman! It's sad, really."

Mrs. Lovely shook her head in disgust. As Frankie moved the needle over the record, Mrs. Lovely held out the whisky bottle to her.

"Here, kid," she said.

"Oh, I couldn't, Mrs. Lovely."

"Go on and live a little, Frankie. I should have given your mom a few swigs at your age. Then she wouldn't be so balled up. Your mother couldn't even handle the glass of champagne at her *wedding*. Dip your feet in the pool of life!"

Frankie grabbed the bottle and gulped. She immediately spewed whisky all over the floor. Embarrassed, she grabbed a towel and began wiping it up.

Mrs. Allen, who was Frankie's third stop, sprang to life. "Speaking of dipping toes in pools," she said, "remember when we took a dip in old man Walker's pond? Naked?"

All the ladies began laughing proudly. "What would I give to be that free now!" Mrs. Lovely said. "Hey, there's a nice fountain at Twilight Time. Maybe we could make a splash again there sometime soon."

The women hooted and hollered. After a bottle of whisky and two packs of cigarettes, the gray haired ladies pranced out of Suzie's salon feeling younger than they had in years. And Frankie had not just witnessed all of this as though from a ringside seat— she had been in the ring with them for all of it!

For the next two years, Frankie spent every Tuesday afternoon at the Gray Haired Speakeasy. It was their wisdom and yearning for fun that forced Frankie to eventually realize she *had* to get out of the small town and into the big city, where fun was all around.

As soon as she was old enough to move away from home, she took off to New York City. Her mother and father didn't speak to her for weeks. They were appalled their little girl would leave Austin, Texas to go to "that filthy city, filled with 'free-love'-ing, druggie hippies."

As she left, they told her she would be miserable there and she would be home in a matter of months. However, Grams knew the truth. That carefree partying attitude she saw come alive in Frankie was there to stay. Frankie was made for a life of fun, and she wouldn't find it unless she got away from her mother and father.

Once she arrived in New York, Frankie immediately found her way. It was everything she'd dreamed of, and she hit the streets running. She auditioned for plays, danced at clubs, and waitressed tables at a diner. What more could one expect from a young girl in New York City?

Disco balls were sparkling and bellbottoms were swinging. She began to frequent Studio 54. The owners, Steve and Ian, loved Frankie's smile and her energy. If someone was dancing, drinking or doing a line with Frankie, they were always happy. There were standing instructions with Mark at the door to let Frankie in . . . *any* night of the week and *any* week of the year. And because Frankie loved the excitement and glamour of Studio 54, she came out as many nights of the week as she possibly could.

One night, after seeing Cher strut into the club, Frankie made her way to the balcony, her mind set on wooing one of her favorite singers. Once she made her way "inside the ropes" to where the stars hung out, the youngster from Austin talked and smiled and enamored her way right into the Goddess of Pop's heart. Cher was so struck with Frankie, they spent two hours dancing.

There were other celebrities, too, who came to be enchanted by her. Even Sylvester Stallone, who never so much as gave anyone in the club a thought, was taken with Frankie. She actually spent a few hours in the VIP lounge with "Rocky." At one point, he demanded that his entourage play "Gonna' Fly Now" as they "did it," flying high themselves.

She may have gotten lost in that year, if it hadn't been for the news that Grams had passed. It hit Frankie like a ton of bricks. That night, in honor of her grandmother, she came to the Studio 54 door dressed in a black flapper dress with a pink feather in her black bobbed wig.

"Trying out a new look tonight, Frankie?" Mark asked.

"Absolutely. Now, be a doll and let me in. It's cold out here tonight!"

He gave her a peck on the cheek and opened the door for her.

"Don't break any hearts tonight!" he called.

"I won't, you ol' sap!"

She made her way to the DJ.

"Frankie! Look at you!"

"Hi, Ducky! I need a favor."

"For you, anything."

"Can you play "Ain't She Sweet for Me"?

"You mean the Beatles song?" he asked. "I don't know if that's gonna' fly here."

"No, silly. I have a record here."

She pulled out a copy of "Ain't She Sweet" by Gene Austin and handed it over. "Wait until I get up on the stage. Then let it play. Oh, and can you direct the spotlight to the stage when the music starts?"

"Okay. But, promise me a drink later?"

"Sure, sure."

Frankie made her way to the stage. "Night Fever" was blaring, as she stared out at the crowd, seeing how happy everyone was here. She contemplated the fact that ninety-nine percent of them were either drunk or high, and thought to herself that most people would be happy under those circumstances. The question was, *what were they like the next morning when they woke up?*

Frankie was naturally almost always happy, oblivious to the problems and worries others faced. This particular night, however, she caught a glimpse of what it was like to be unhappy. Grams was gone. She would never see her again. And that weighed on her heart, even as she stood there onstage. But life *does* move on. That is what Grams would tell her. There was only one thing she could do.

As "Night Fever" faded, she heard the scratchy music begin. Closing her eyes for a moment, Frankie took a deep breath. She pictured the smile on Grams's face as she listened to her music. Then, she let the music take over.

All the gold lame and sequins froze on the dance floor. The disco ball was still spinning, but the crowd stopped in confusion. Frankie pranced out to the front of the stage and with the spotlight right on her, she began dancing the Charleston! She danced with her heart and soul. Her legs were swinging and the fringe on her dress was swaying. Within moments, a wild grin broke out on her face.

The DJ took a deep breath and scanned the audience for Ian, the owner. But as he did, he noticed the crowd was starting to move with Frankie. As she pursed her lips and flung her arms to the side, everyone on the dance floor began to copy her steps. As crazy as it sounds, Liza Minnelli happened to be there, and *she* jumped up onstage with Frankie and began dancing right along with her. It was one of those moments never seen before or after at Studio 54. The place had gotten swept up by Frankie's unorthodox, energized tribute to Grams.

And as the music began to fade, the applause began . . . and continued . . . for a whole minute! Frankie took a big bow, all the while holding Liza's hand in hers.

Ian was just reaching the DJ booth, as Frankie made her way down the stairs. "So help me God, did you do this?" he asked Frankie.

"Of course! You don't think your DJ would have done something like this on his own, do you? You're not mad are you? The crowd loved it!" She gave him a cute pout and kissed his cheek, leaving a big red lip stamp on his cheek.

"Only for you, Frankie! Only for you! Next time, just run it by me first. Okay?" Realizing he'd made his point and no harm had been done, he shifted gears. "Now listen, you want to party with us in the basement?"

"Sure. I'll be along! Gimme' a minute!"

Frankie made her way to the exit and walked out into the cold night air. Her feather was blowing in the brisk New York City wind. Hailing a taxi, she climbed in, told the driver her apartment address, pulled away from Studio 54 for the last time. Frankie had decided it was time to move on . . . to find the next party in her life.

Luckily for her, she met Ed three days later in the diner. He was a stockbroker on Wall Street, and a regular at the diner, where he watched her every time she went to refill anyone's coffee. That day, when he left, he wrote his phone number on a hundred dollar bill he left her for a tip.

That had been a little over the top, in Frankie's eyes. She wasn't for sale. But she remembered he had nice eyes and good vibes, not that creepy sort of vibe a lot of the guys in the diner had when they were hitting on her. Later that night, she decided to give him a call, since she didn't have anywhere else to be.

A couple nights later, as they drank a bottle of champagne and enjoyed a lobster dinner, Frankie realized Ed was an easygoing sort of guy. She had worried he might be uptight, what with his stock market job. However, Ed showed an affinity for fun as much as for work. He loved partying, too, she discovered quickly. He just frequented the more upscale social parties in New York. Frankie was all for joining him, though. In short time, they became known as one of New York's most fun-loving couples.

Not six months later, after throwing a wedding with a reception that lasted long into the night, Frankie and Ed enjoyed the night life at its best: opening night parties, museum galas, brokerage firm parties and close friends' Christmas parties. After two years, Frankie decided the next kind of party she wanted was a baby shower.

"Ed, darling," she began, after they returned from dinner one night, "I've been thinking about how wonderful it would be to have a little Ed around. Just imagine it! A little Ed, followed by Lillian, named after Grams. Our family would be the envy of all our friends. We'll have amazing birthday parties! Lillian's wedding will be the most fun wedding this old town has ever seen! What do you say?"

Ed gazed into her excited eyes and enjoyed her vision as much as she did. By this time, they were financially stable, and Ed was moving along quite well in his career. "Of course, Frankie. I can't think of anything I would want more."

For six years, Ed and Frankie tried to have a baby. With each passing month, Frankie became more and more desperate. She also began to throw more and more parties. It was the only thing that took her mind off her disappointment. She became New York's source for all things "party." Even the second and third generation socialites called on Frankie for advice or ideas when giving a big soiree.

Finally, in the spring of 1986, Frankie sent out the invitations she had dreamed of for years. Seventy-five of their closest friends received delivery of a big fluffy teddy bear with a red ribbon tied around its neck. On the ribbon was a bright white stationary heart that read, "Ed and Frankie would like for you to join them on Friday, April 2nd at 8:00 pm."

On the appointed day, their apartment was filled with pastel balloons and teddy bears. Champagne was served in crystal glasses, each adorned with a pastel ribbon. Lullabies were playing on the sound system. A five-course meal was served. As the petit fours were passed for dessert, the formal announcement was made. Of course, after the guests saw Frankie's glow and Ed's pride, the news was out the minute they walked through the door. "We're having a baby!" she squealed.

The pregnancy moved along fine, until the fourth month. One morning, Frankie went to the bathroom and noticed some spotting. She drove herself to the OB/GYN, since she was sure everything would be fine. She and Ed were going to the opening of a new art gallery that evening. As the nurses performed a sonogram, they realized the baby's heart wasn't beating. Frankie was admitted to the hospital and Ed was called. She was taken into surgery and an emergency hysterectomy was performed.

When Ed walked into the hospital room, it was the first time he could ever recall seeing Frankie look truly and dismally sad. As she locked eyes with him, she began crying uncontrollably. She cried all through that day and the night. As she slept, Frankie had a dream about Grams, who was sitting on a chaise lounge smoking a cigarette. She looked just like she had during her heyday, all rouged up and dressed to the hilt. Grams looked at Frankie with love in her eyes.

"Cheer up, Duckie. All will be okay. Life is just one party after another. Don't let the tragedy get in the way of fun!"

Frankie woke up and called Vince, one of New York's premier party planners. She normally only called Vince when she was throwing a party so big she couldn't handle it on her own. The party she was planning wasn't big; nevertheless, she couldn't handle it. She knew Vince could be counted on. That afternoon, at 4:00, Father Al walked into room 346 and saw a view that would have made the Virgin Mary weep.

Frankie was dressed in a black silk dressing gown. Ed was seated next to her on a chair in a black suit. There were a handful of guests standing about. There was a small buffet near the window, filled with small sandwiches, a silver coffee service and an ice bucket with a bottle of white wine. A small silver box was lying on the bed surrounded by rattles, teddy bears and other cuddly stuffed animals. Engraved on the lid were the words, "May Our Little Angel Rest in the Arms of the Blessed Mother." White roses filled vases all around the room.

Frankie, although trying to appear stoic, was wiping away her tears, as she saw the priest enter the room. She immediately walked to him and hugged him, the way a little girl hugs her father when she is hurt. He was taken aback, but what could he do other than embrace her and try to console her.

"Don't cry, my child. He is in God's hands, now."

Frankie sobbed at least another half hour, while the other guests looked on with pity in their eyes. When she felt as though there were no more tears to be shed, she wiped her eyes and excused herself to the bathroom. Touching up her make-up and straightening her robe, she exited the bathroom with a smile on her face.

"Thank you all for coming to support Ed and I. I wanted to send our little baby into God's arms filled with warmth and love. I wanted him to feel how loved he is."

She leaned over and kissed the tiny silver coffin, then motioned to Father Al, who began the saying the rosary.

Frankie picked herself up by the bootstraps, as Grams would say, and continued her life. She and Ed traveled the world and never sat still for long. Nothing held them back from a life of fun. Ed had made a lot of money over the years, and was fortunate enough to retire at 60. He and Frankie moved to Florida.

Frankie had big plans. They were going to join the local country club. She would plan tennis matches, with brunch soirees afterwards at their new home. She would throw luaus in the summer by their beautiful new pool. She would host poker nights for Ed and the many golfing buddies he would meet. Leaving New York was easier, when she thought of all the new parties she would throw.

They spent one night in their new home. At 9:30 the next morning, they were going to meet an interior designer to discuss plans for the kitchen. When Frankie went upstairs with a cup of coffee for Ed, she found him on the bathroom floor. She dropped the coffee cup and splashed hot coffee on her legs, fell down at his side and grabbed his arm. Ed's body was cold. She lay next to him and pressed her burning legs next to his cool body for a long time and cried.

Now, here she was, five years later, alone. Frankie didn't make it to the country club. She didn't make it to the garden circle. She barely made it to the grocery store. She waited for it to get easier. As she stared out at the hibiscus bush, she wondered what it would look like decorated in twinkling lights. She pictured tropical fruit centerpieces scattered on the patio furniture. She could almost see the floating candles twinkling in the pool. Yes, she would ask the prayer lady to pray for a party.

9 HEAVENLY VISIONS & STRANDS OF HAIR

Havin' Wayne know about my prayer business has actually been better than I thought it would be. It's nice to have someone to talk to about it. I know that talking to God should be enough, but God ain't so quick to chit-chat about this person or that person, like Wayne. I also think it does Wayne some good to know that prayers are real important. I don't know how much he prays. He doesn't really go to church. Seems he always has a job or something that keeps him busy on Sunday mornin's. Every day that I sit in church by myself, I just remember first Corinthians 7:13: "If any woman has a husband who is an unbeliever, and he consents to live with her, she should not divorce him. For the unbelieving husband is made holy because of his wife, and the unbelieving wife is made holy because of her husband." I know we ain't married yet, but I think by being a good

Christian woman, I am already helpin' him become a better man for Jesus.

I wondered if he might want to help me pray for my newest client. I figured the more he prayed, the more he would get to know Jesus. So, I read him the email from Trenton. Seems he wants me to pray that his friend, Johnny, finds a girl he saw in a vision. He asked me if I needed a strand of his hair, though. I don't know what to make of that. I let him know that no hair was necessary — just payment to my Paypal account.

I had a vision once when I was thirteen. I was swinging on the swings at my school. There was a cool breeze blowin' and I could hear church bells ringin' in the distance. A bright light came up in front of my eyes, so bright I couldn't make out anything else around me. There was a shadow that drifted into the light. It was the shape of a person. That was all I could see. I just sat on that swing, starin' into the light, until my teacher yelled for us to come inside. I blinked and the light was gone. I never told anyone else about it. Of course, as the years go by, I wonder if maybe I was just about to swing myself to sleep. Maybe it was the sun shinin' so bright, it blinded me for a minute. But when I let myself wander right back to that time in my mind, I know it was God, or maybe an angel. I figure if Johnny's vision was from God, it must be pretty important.

Wayne told me he ain't ever had a vision or anything like that. He figures he ain't holy enough. I know he ain't the most religious man, but I know I can bring him around.

10 JOHNNY AND THE FACE

Johnny went to the University of Florida, and graduated with a degree in architecture. As a child, he loved to build model cars and often designed whole cities with Legos. There was really no doubt in his mind that architecture was his destiny. However, the economic downfall was making his destiny very hard to reach. Luckily, Johnny had a nice trust fund and very understanding parents. He buckled down and decided to wait for the turning tides that eventually *had* to bring the economy back to its feet.

Most of his other fraternity buddies had jobs lined up months before graduation. However, his best friend, Trenton, had bucked the conventional job market and decided there was only one way to land the job of his dreams, the job that would provide him with creative license, boatloads of dough, and freedom. Knowing Johnny was footloose and fancy-free, Trenton coerced him into delving into the world of independent films. Of course, he felt that independent films would eventually lead him into Steven Spielberg status. However, one had to have a place to start. Thus began Trenton and Johnny's first independent documentary film, _Reservations, My Ass._

Johnny was actually as excited about the endeavor as Trenton. He had even invested in the film. Their budget was super-low, because there wouldn't be a need for lights, fancy cameras and heavy-duty sound equipment. Since Johnny and Trenton would be starring in the film, they also didn't have to worry about paying for talent. What required money was the Bentley rental, the Gucci suits and the expensive restaurant tabs.

The film's premise was simple, actually. The idea had come to Trenton when he visited Miami—South Beach, to be exact. He had followed a gorgeous girl who was walking down Collins Avenue. When she dipped into a frou-frou restaurant, Trenton followed. The woman got a table on the patio right away, but Trenton was denied access to the restaurant. The maître d', a thirty-something woman wearing a tight-fitting black dress, told him the tables were all booked. At first, he blamed his khaki shorts and flip-flops, but as he scanned the patio, he saw there were others wearing shorts. In South Beach, shorts are never denied. He also noticed there were _many_ empty tables. As the hostess snubbed her nose at him, Trenton realized he wasn't cool or suave enough to partake in a meal at this upscale Miami restaurant. However, although he was slightly overweight, a little clumsy and hadn't brushed his hair that morning, he was still a person. He wondered how many tourists or lower class Miami citizens were turned away each day. *Funny, Trenton thought, how someone making little more than minimum wage working a hostess stand gets to decide who is worthy enough to dine at an establishment.*

That's when his idea was born. He decided to show the shallowness of maître d's and restaurants all over the country. Many of them only let in those they thought were worthy, judging by their clothes or the car they arrived in. What about those millionaires who didn't really give a damn what anyone thought of them and made no effort to look wealthy? What about those who live in a one-bedroom apartment, and max out their credit cards for expensive clothes? In Trenton's eyes, *everyone* should be treated as equals. But, his experience showed him that maître d's often felt they needed to snub diners.

Johnny had immediately been game for Trenton's venture. Although he'd never been denied access into an establishment, he hated the airs that maître d's put on. *Really, what's the point in trying to make someone feel inadequate?* Johnny thought. Anyway, he had jumped at the chance to travel the country with Trenton. What else did he have to do until the housing market came back?

Their first stop was back to the same restaurant in South Beach that had snubbed Trenton. They rented a beautiful black Bentley and Johnny wore a perfectly fitted Armani suit, along with a fake Rolex, dripping in what looked just like real diamonds. His alligator shoes and Gucci shades exuded an air of money, and he slicked his wavy black hair back with just enough gel, so as not to look greasy.

The only thing bigger than Trenton's personality was his girth. At 6'6" and 280 pounds, his suit was somewhat larger and less fitted than Johnny's. He also wore shades, a hat and carried an airsoft gun strapped to a harness under his blazer.

They waited until Friday night at 8:00 to make their stop. This particular restaurant was booked for three months in advance on weekend nights, following a million-dollar renovation and a story on the Leisure Network. Their first stop would decide whether Trenton and Johnny's project had any merit.

Trenton pulled the Bentley up to the front door of the restaurant. As luck would have it, he noticed the same woman was working the front door.

"Go time," he said to Johnny, as he exited the car.

He adjusted the hat on his head which concealed a hidden video camera. Trenton adjusted his earpiece and exited the car, standing on the sidewalk with his arms crossed over his chest. He scanned the street and sidewalk, as though looking for any danger that might be lurking in front of him. He then looked at the maître d' and noticed she was eyeing him with interest.

He raised his wrist to his mouth and spoke into his watch, "Coast is clear, Sir."

He then raised the watch to his ear and nodded. He walked toward the desk and without taking his glasses off, he nodded solemnly at the maître d'.

"Good day, ma'am. I need a table for one please . . . in a *private* area. I would also like to speak with the manager of this establishment. I need the utmost discretion, and it's imperative no media be alerted."

The woman nodded excitedly and stared at the Bentley — no doubt trying to make out the face behind the tinted glass.

"And the name, please?" she asked while still straining to see through the dark glass.

"Let just say it is . . . Mr. Jones," he replied with a wink.

Her eyebrows knitted together and then shot up. She nodded in a conspiratorial way.

"Ah, Mr. Jones. Yes, I will have a table ready in a few moments. The manager is already on his way up. Just a moment, please."

Johnny, who was sitting in the car watching, wished that the Timex on Trenton's arm really *was* a two-way radio. He would have loved to have known what was being said. However, he could tell from the expressions on the maître d's face, they were in. Soon, a flustered looking man walked to the desk. He was bobbing his head up and down, as Trenton talked. A woman in an apron approached, followed by a man in a chef's hat. Trenton really had them jumping.

After about five minutes, Trenton returned to the car. He handed the valet attendant a fifty-dollar bill and opened the door for Johnny. Johnny sauntered into the restaurant with his cell to his ear. He acted as if there was no one in the establishment but himself. As he arrived at his table, there was a bottle of Dom and a Bud Light on ice. It was everything he could do to keep a straight face. Closing his cell-phone, Johnny noticed all conversation had stopped, and waiters and waitresses were scurrying to his table delivering ice water, bread with butter, and the restaurant's signature crab legs.

Trenton pulled out the chair for Johnny, who sat quietly and feigned boredom. After a few minutes, he whispered to Trenton. "Hey, aren't you even going to sit down?"

"No, man, I'm your body guard. I have to be on my toes. I also have a better view with the hat camera if I'm standing."

Johnny glanced around. The activity around their table had slowed somewhat.

"What if they figure out I'm a nobody?"

"Don't worry. I've got it covered. I paid a guy at the bar next door to barge onto the patio with a camera, if I call his cell-phone. That should squelch any ideas you aren't a celeb."

With that, Johnny decided to sit back and enjoy his lunch — the Dom chased by the Bud, followed by about a dozen crab legs.

"Hey, Trenton. Next time, maybe we should switch roles. You're really missing out, here."

"No, man. I ain't missing nothing! A small town New Orleans boy on the verge of winning the Sundance. I'm all good."

They didn't even have to call on the man at the bar. Things went so smoothly that the manager thanked Johnny and offered his meal to him with no charge. He asked only that they visit again.

Their next stop would be a steak house in Dallas that catered to oil tycoons. However, Johnny had planned to join his father, a University of Florida Bullgator, in the box for the Florida/Tennessee football game. Trenton was obligated to attend a cousin's wedding in Baton Rouge. It was decided Johnny would drive to New Orleans after the game on Saturday.

Trenton would meet up with him after the wedding. They figured a night on Bourbon Street was in order, before they made the trip to Dallas.

Johnny left after the football game at around 7:30. He figured he would drive through the night when traffic was slow. He was young and staying up late was nothing to him. He loaded up his car before the game and left directly after. He had tailgated for a few hours before the game, but he figured that sitting in the Florida heat sweating like a pig would burn off most of the alcohol. As Johnny got onto Interstate 75, he felt just a little buzz. He drove on for a few hours without any trouble at all. Traffic was light, and he found a McDonald's just about the time his stomach started growling. After a Big Mac, medium fries and a large chocolate shake, he was ready to lay some more miles down.

As time wore on, the roads got darker and longer. There were quite a few back roads he had to drive in order to reach New Orleans. Usually, Johnny liked these drives. He felt like time had stopped in these rural areas. He imagined another time, another place, far away from the hustle and bustle of campus life. He supposed that was where his mind was when he drove through the stop sign. He had been watching a bird fly overhead in the moonlight. Dave Matthews was playing on the radio and his mind was a million miles away. Running the stop sign itself wasn't the problem. Earlier, he'd been worried about one of these small town hick cops pulling him over and smelling the alcohol from the day's game on his breath. He had heard policemen in country towns like this didn't have much sympathy for city boys.

Johnny noticed the stop sign just as he passed it going sixty miles an hour. He was looking all around for the red and blue flashing lights. He peered over his shoulder and was just about to breathe a sigh of relief, when a wild turkey walked out of the woods to his right and strutted smack dab into the middle of the road. As Johnny spied it, it was surreal. His first thought was that Thanksgiving was still a few months away. Then he suddenly remembered a smoked turkey his Grandfather had made years earlier. By far, it was the best Thanksgiving bird he had ever had the pleasure of eating. But these thoughts fluttered away quickly, as he realized the bird was just standing right in the middle of the road. Shocked, he supposed. He honked his horn and began to brake, but the bird just stared at him with his waddle quivering. Johnny made the decision to swerve to the right, hoping that the turkey would continue to make his way to the left side of the road. With a split second to spare, he swerved to the right shoulder, only to see the turkey had decided to go back the way he came. With a quick turn of the wheel to the left, he missed the turkey, who strutted into the woods gobbling angrily.

Johny's car flipped twice and came to rest in a ditch on the side of the road. One can never really be prepared for the feeling of being tossed around inside a car that's spinning out of control. As it was happening, he didn't see his life flash before his eyes, as some report. He was actually thinking about the Gravitron at the county fair his mother took him to when he was eleven. As the car first started to spin, he was pinned to the seat, just as he had been pinned to the spinning walls of the Gravitron. However, as the speed reduced, the crashing pain and the loud sound of metal scraping concrete was like nothing he had ever experienced. He wondered if the seatbelt would do its job, like the public safety announcement promised. As he realized the car had spent all of its energy, he braced himself for the end. He didn't really remember the end, though. Everything went black. Then everything went white.

He tried to open his eyes. Were they open? He wasn't sure. But he could see a beautiful girl staring at him. She was one of the most alluring girls he had ever seen. She touched his arm and smiled at him. *I must look like an idiot,* he thought. Johnny tried to get up, but realized that indeed, the seatbelt was still snuggly fastened across his midsection. She had the most startling brown eyes. He felt like she was peering into his soul. He tried to talk, but nothing came out. Her wispy hair was blowing from her eyes. She smelled like vanilla.

He hadn't even realized that the iPod was still playing through the car stereo. "Crash into me, baby, and I come into you." *You have to love Dave Matthews,* he thought. He realized he had closed his eyes and couldn't see her anymore. He began to panic and forced his eyelids to open. She was still there. *She can't be a dream,* he thought. She took a step back from the car, and he realized he should get out and at least introduce himself. He reached over to unbuckle the seatbelt and fell like a ragdoll onto the side door. He pulled himself up and opened the door. As he exited the car, he realized two things. Number one was that the girl wasn't real. Number two was the excruciating pain in his back. That is what brought him around to his senses. There was no girl—just the pain shooting through his back. He began to walk down the road. Tears were streaming down his face; and with every step he took, he was sure it might be his last.

For one half of a mile, Johnny walked, until he saw a small house with a light on inside. Not a light, he recognized on second glance, but the blue glow of a television set. He banged on the door and yelled for help. Emaline Walker opened the door with a shotgun pointed at Johnny's face. But he collapsed without one single shot being fired.

Emaline called the paramedics and they took him to County Hospital. He had a broken back, contusions on his left side and a concussion. Johnny didn't remember the ride to the hospital in the back of the ambulance. He didn't remember the doctors x-raying him or doing surgery on his back. No, when he woke up, all he remembered was the face. For twenty-four hours, he floated in and out of consciousness, trying to visualize that fetching woman's face again, searching his muddled mind for a clue as to who she was.

Trenton came bounding into the hospital room two days after the accident. Johnny was alert now, just feeling as though his body had been thrown from a train. He was in a back and neck brace and wasn't able to move his torso at all. He heard Trenton's heavy steps before he even reached the room.

"Hey, Johnny!" he exclaimed as he walked into the room. "Why did the turkey cross the road?"

"Very funny. This is all *your* fault, you know. You promise me a good time in the Big Easy and I get nothing but a big pain in the ass . . . and the back, and the neck, and the arm."

"Yeah, yeah. I hear the violins strumming."

Trenton sat on the edge of the bed. "Seriously, buddy. How you holding up? I was ready to call you and give you a piece of my mind, when you still weren't in New Orleans by yesterday morning. I would have been here sooner, if I had known."

"I know. I was just out of it for a while, probably a good thing. They got some good drugs into me before I woke up."

"I talked to your parents. They called to let me know what had happened. They get here yet?"

"Yeah, they're checking into their hotel and coming back after dinner."

He thought again for the thousandth time that day about the girl he had seen. He wondered whether Trenton could be serious long enough to listen to the story. He decided to give it a try. As he finished explaining everything, he started to feel a little foolish. He stared at Trenton and waited for the joke. There was no joke, though. Trenton shook his head, as if it all made perfect sense.

"You know what you have to do, right?" he asked.

Johnny shook his head.

"You have to find her. That's it. That's why the turkey crossed the road. So you could find 'the one.'"

"What do you mean 'find the one'? "

"She was beautiful, you can't stop thinking about her, and she may have even saved your life. If you hadn't seen her and tried to get out of the car, you might have- . . ." he gulped and his eyes began to tear up. "You know, you might not be here now. She is your soul mate. We just *have* to find her."

"It was just a dream, though," Johnny replied. "I was unconscious. Obviously, there really was nobody there. Why would I think about somebody I don't even know? Somebody I may not have even really seen before!"

"Because it's the *universe* talking to you. It got your attention by throwing the turkey in your path. Once it had you thinking of nothing else, it showed you someone, someone special. Now, it's up to you."

"Jeez, Trenton, I didn't know you were so deep."

"Hey, I took philosophy my sophomore year. I also had a grandmother deep in the Bayou who could talk to the birds and cure illnesses with swamp plants. I believe in all kinds of shit."

"Can these swamp plants help to figure out who this is?"

"Well, the swamp plants won't do much, unless you have a cold or a fever. But a good voodoo priest or priestess will find your girl. Their magic stuff *works*. There was one who lived next door to my grandmother when I was growing up. She always knew everything. This one time, I stole a pack of cigarettes from the store. I'd grabbed my grandmother's box of matches and tucked them, along with the cigarettes, into my sweatshirt pocket. I was going to hide back in the woods and try my hand at smoking. Just as I was walking out the door, I saw the voodoo lady was standing on the porch. I nearly shit my pants. She was really spooky looking. Anyway, she looked at me and I'll never forget what she said. She said, 'Smokey, smokey, won't you, boy. Black will be your lungs. From this naughty ploy, your ruin will be spung.'"

"Oh my God, what'd you do?"

"I just said, "Yes, ma'am." She held out her gnarled fingers, and I put the cigarettes in them then I ran inside and locked the door. I watched her walk back down the dirt road to her house. She sat on the front porch and must have smoked every last one of those cigarettes. I don't know what would have happened had I smoked them. That curse scared me so bad, I've still never touched a cigarette."

"You're full of shit."

Trenton pulled out his iPhone. "Let's see, what shall we search? Find a missing person, visions, true love, voodoo, or how about prayers?" he continued to stare at the phone in silence for a few more minutes, before jumping up.

"I've got it! Here's a voodoo priestess who promises to find your true love. All you have to do is send her a strand of your hair!"

Johnny rolled his eyes. "You're nuts. I'm not sending my hair to a voodoo wizard or whatever you said."

"Okay, I see, the voodoo route isn't for you. Okay, no problem," he said, as he continued his online search.

"Alright, this seems to be more your speed. A prayer lady. She'll pray for you seven times a day. If that doesn't help us find this girl, I don't know what will."

Trenton immediately sent a payment to her Paypal account. He turned his phone towards Johnny.

"Here, now we just wait. This is your receipt. I'll email it to you."

"What the hell? I can't believe you just wasted your money like that."

"Just wait. We'll find your girl. You just have to get yourself better. Rest and get out of this damn bed, you hear me? I need my best friend."

Trenton's eyes teared up again. Johnny shook his head and closed his eyes. He needed a nap. The last thing that crossed his mind as he drifted into sleep was that woman's big brown eyes.

11 ONWARD CHRISTIAN SOLDIERS

I near about cried all day yesterday. I don't usually cry. I just take my burdens to Jesus, and I let him wash them away. But yesterday, I cried enough tears to wash away the sins of most everybody in town. I went over to the church to help Mrs. Whipple put the fall colored candles in the church. She couldn't stand up well enough to reach the candelabras on the altar. I have to stand on a chair myself to reach 'em. Anyway, after taking direction from Mrs. Whipple, who was stuck at the back of the church, on account of her scooter still wouldn't fit down the aisles, I needed to get home. My client load was pretty heavy, and Drew from Ware State Prison and I usually had one of our weekly chats on the computer on Thursdays. I had a lot do to. So, I helped her over to the church office, where she liked to hang out with the Reverend and his secretary, Patsy. I heard crying and carryin' on from behind Reverend Sander's closed door. Patsy had her rollin' chair over near the file cabinet right outside the office, and

100

was leanin' so close to the door that the chair looked like it could tip at any minute. When we walked in, she straightened up quick and rolled her chair back to her desk.

"Oh, hey there, Grace," Patsy said with a nod. "You're looking good this mornin'," she said to Mrs. Whipple, as she patted her hand.

Now, Mrs. Whipple loves to be in the know, just as much as Patsy – I reckon that's why she sometimes likes to hang out in the church office – so I figured I best get on out of there. It was none of their business who was cryin' to Reverend Sanders, and it sure wadn't none of mine. As I was politely makin' my excuse to leave, the Reverend's door opened. He walked out with a grave look on his face. Behind him, came a tear-streaked Mandy and Wayne with his arm around her. He was just a-pattin' her shoulders and consolin' her with all that charm of his.

"We can't think of this as a punishment for our sins," he was sayin'. "We have to remember that God has a plan for all of us, and as surprising and upsetting as this may seem, it is his will. So, we will get through this."

Mandy looked plain green. She was holdin' her stomach. In that moment of weakness, all I could think of was that she was pregnant. And seein' Wayne standin' there with his arm around her, I had a real good idea that he was the daddy. I turned and ran out of that building faster than I ever moved. Out of the corner of my eye, I saw Wayne trying to get to me, but I wadn't about to let him anywhere near me ever again.

I got home and locked the doors, which I don't ever do. Wayne called over and over, but I didn't answer. I had to pray. I had a job that decent folks were payin' me for. But first, I had to ask God to forgive the hate that was bubblin' up inside of me. How could Wayne do this to me? God had handpicked us to be together, but Wayne didn't care. I should have known he was a good-for-nothin'! But God had sent him.

He showed up at the trailer about a half an hour later. He banged on the door and begged to explain. I couldn't handle it anymore. I wanted to yell at him and I wanted to hear his excuse. I wanted to know why he would hurt me like this. I looked over at the clock. It was almost 2:30. I took a big breath and walked over to the door and thought better about opening it. So I went over to the bathroom and pulled the little window up.

"Wayne, I've got a job that I'm tryin' to do. You come back in an hour and I'll listen to you. Hear me?"

"Okay, baby," he said. "I'll come back. You just have to let me explain what happened. It's not what you think."

"Go on, now! I cain't listen to you, now."

I went back in and said a quick prayer and asked God to just get me through the day. Then I spent the next half hour prayin' for my clients. I could barely get through a prayer without thinking about Wayne and Mandy. By the time he showed up, I had calmed down a bit. I let him in the trailer, but I didn't offer him a glass of tea or nothin'. He looked real nervous. I was glad to see him squirm.

"You go on, now. Tell me whatever it is you got to say."

"Baby, I don't know what you think you saw, but it was just a big old mistake! Mandy's hot water heater broke a few days back, and she asked me to come over and fix it for her . . . as a payin' customer, that's all! But when I got to her house, she was standin' out in the front yard cryin'. Baby, you ain't gonna' believe this, but painted, right on her front door, was a pentegram."

I wadn't quite sure what that was, and it must have shown on my face, because Wayne went right on explainin'.

"A pentagram is the symbol for Satan. Somebody here in our town is worshipin' Satan, and they are tryin' to spread it around."

"What? You mean there ain't nothin' going on with you two?"

"No, baby. Nothin' more than a friend helpin' out a friend! Mandy just thought somebody didn't like her and was tryin' to make fun of her, til' I explained that the symbol was the symbol used by those worshipin' the Devil himself. After I scrubbed the paint off the door, she got dressed and asked if I would take her over to see Reverend Sanders. She was in no condition to drive. So I took her to the church, and we told Reverend Sanders what happened. That's all, darlin'. I promise!"

You know those times in your life when you're truly ashamed of yourself? Those times you wish you could go back and erase? This was one of those times. I grabbed Wayne around the neck and hugged him like there wadn't no tomorrow. Of course he hadn't forsaken me! He was the man God sent for me, and I was bein' too stupid to remember it. After apologizing and promising that I wouldn't doubt him again, I got to thinkin' more about the pentagram.

"What did the Reverend say?"

"Well, he said that hopefully it was just some teenagers tryin' to play a joke on Mandy . . . just bein' funny. But we're supposed to keep our eyes open for any more signs. I reckon some of your prayers would help, too."

I gladly prayed, right then and there, for the poor souls who were playin' with fire hotter than they realized. Wayne seemed awful relieved I was talkin' to him again, and I gotta' admit it was nice to be havin' his arms around me again. Everything went fine for a few more days, until Mrs. Whipple pulled her scooter out of the garage. She was going to let her dog, LuLu, out, and as she rolled the scooter onto her driveway, there was another pentagram. She called the police, the Reverend, her son, and Wayne, just because she wanted what she called "the filth" cleaned up right away. There was quite a ruckus over at her house.

As it happened, Marla Jones lived next door to Mrs. Whipple. She was a reporter for the Daily Times, our town newspaper. Wayne said she came over with a notebook and a pencil and started asking all kind of questions. The police chief pulled her aside and asked if she was going to write up a story to go in the next day's paper. When she said yes, he asked if she might put it off until one more incident happened. Wayne said the chief was worried about starting a panic over a prank. Marla agreed, but the story went to press the followin' evenin', on account of the pentagram that appeared on the door of the Sunny Day Diner. By the time the story came out, most everyone in town already knew about what was happening. However, not only did the story show up in the Daily Times, it showed up in every paper and on the news in all the counties around us. There was a panic . . . and it turned right quick into a real epidemic.

Reverend Sanders called a special meeting of the church council to talk about what Eden Baptist Church could do. I was on the council, so I made sure I didn't miss that meeting. I didn't like the thought of Devil worshipers walking around our town. Over the next few weeks, everyone seemed to be on edge. We was all lookin' at each other, tryin' to see who looked like they had evil lurking in 'em. I also looked around the church real good the following Sunday to see who wadn't there. I figured that if Lucifer took hold of your heart, he wouldn't let you anywhere near a church where good folks could help you find salvation.

The only person I could tell was missin' was Silas Finnegan and Bilbo Cousins. They went missin' somewhat regularly, though, on account of hunting season. They go deer hunting a lot and make the best venison jerky you've ever eaten! I hoped they were just hunting deer to make jerky, and not killin' animals as sacrifices to the Devil.

The other thing that made me and the other folks on the council nervous was that Halloween was just around the corner. Halloween is usually just a fun time in our town. Of course, what little one doesn't like to dress up and get candy? But with the fear of the Devil risin' up, we started wonderin' whether or not celebratin' on this day was such a good idea. Reverend Sanders urged all the committee members to research and pray about how to handle Halloween.

I did my fair share of internet searching on the subject. In just a few hours, I learned all kind of stuff. Many rock stars have sold their souls to the Devil. A famous company, which I don't want to spread rumors about, gives most of its profits to the Satanist church. Many Devil worshipers perform ceremonies on Halloween night. The most disturbin' thing I found was that some of Lucifer's followers put razor blades and poison in candy to be given out to trick-or-treaters. That was enough to really scare me!

Wayne got scared, too, because he came to me with a worried look on his face, tellin' me he just didn't like the thought of any Satanist bein' around. He suggested I ought to put an ad in the local papers advertisin' my prayer services, since there were likely to be so many good people who needed a little extra protection. I decided he was right. So I took out ads in the Daily Times and the other papers in the seven counties closest to us. I figured nothin' much would come of it, but I wanted to help whoever I could. I actually got a lot of emails after that ad. When people worry about Satan comin' to their town, they are more willing to pay for prayers.

When the council met again, we decided to urge the church and the community to skip trick-or-treating altogether this year. I felt real bad for the little ones. I said a special prayer asking God to make it easier on them. As I woke up the next morning, it hit me: Ephesians 6:11 — "Put on the full armor of God, so that you can take your stand against the Devil's schemes."

I called Wayne that morning, and he was as happy as a clam to help me with my plan. Reverend Sanders was real excited, too. I even called upon Mandy and the quiltin' group. She was still so shook up about the sign on her door that she was more than happy to pitch in. She was even nice to me. The quiltin' ladies spent the next two weeks making the armor with cardboard and silver spray paint.

When Halloween came around, every child I knew came marchin' up to the church in their costumes. "Onward Christian Soldiers" played real loud on the speakers that Wayne had helped wire. The sight of all those precious little ones, God's own little army, marching towards me gave me the chills.

I stood outside in the front of the sanctuary along with the rest of the church committee. We were decked out in the costumes we used each year at Christmas. Wayne had built us a new stable, and there we were. The nativity scene was complete, down to the lambs and the wise men. The only thing missin' was the baby Jesus. It would be two more months until he arrived. For now, the cradle was overflowing with candy. There were Butterfingers, Gobstoppers, lollipops, bubblegum, popcorn balls, and Mrs. Whipple's famous caramel apples. The children marched up, one-by-one, and filled up their bags with candy from Jesus's cradle to remind them God would always provide for them, even in times of trouble.

I smiled so much that night, my cheeks hurt. Wayne gave me a big kiss on the forehead after the last of the children had gone off to explore their candy.

"You did good, babe," he said.

"You did good, too. Without this new stable and the music, it wouldn't have been nearly as festive. Thank you."

I said it to him as much as I said it to God. I wanted him to know how thankful I was that he'd answered my prayers.

12 Tampon Lillies and the Promised Land

The Humbolt Bible Extravaganza Parade was approaching quickly. Cindy was almost done with her float. The Garden of Gethsemane was alive with inspiration. However, the boxes Uncle Ricky had given to Cindy with returned or damaged merchandise had seemed impossible to work with in the beginning.

"Uncle Ricky, what am I supposed to do with two dozen cartons of tampons?"

He seemed slightly embarrassed. "I'm not sure, sugar. I guess I should have thrown those out. They were shipped by mistake and were just sitting in the back room. I thought that with your imagination, you might be able to figure something out."

Cindy was on her way to toss the big boxes into the dumpster when an idea hit her.

Now, the day before the parade, she stood next to the float, smiling at her own ingenuity. The Garden of

108

Gethsemane was blooming with tampon Easter lilies. Once the cardboard was removed and the cotton was opened, it only took some yellow paint, a couple snips with scissors and a little tweaking to turn those feminine products into the most beautiful flowers you would ever want to see.

The Women's Circle might have junk from the bazaar, but I've got tampons! Cindy thought.

She had solicited the help of a few friends in putting together the float. It struck Cindy as funny that the boys flat-out refused to work on the lilies. There was plenty of other work to go around, though. The gnarled olive trees had to be plastered and painted. Another group was painting the banner, which would hang from the side of the float. It read, "Then he said to them, 'My soul is overwhelmed with sorrow to the point of death. Stay here and keep watch with me.' Matthew 26:39."

The final fitting for the robes was at 4:00. She tried to talk her best friend, Gillian, into doing it. But there was no getting through to her. Nobody wanted to have to wrap Luke in the burlap. It was too much of a temptation. He was the Jesus who everyone fought over each year. His coloring was perfect. His hair was perfect. His eyes were perfect. Nowhere in Humboldt, hell, probably nowhere in *Kansas*, could you find a better Jesus. Cindy couldn't believe that he hadn't already been asked to be in the parade this year. She really lucked out, she thought, when he came into the drug store for conditioner and toilet bowl cleaner the day after last year's parade. When he placed his items on the counter, it startled Cindy. She had been thinking of an Oprah episode she had seen earlier in the week. But she jumped as she snapped to.

"Oh God, you scared me!"

"Not God, Jesus," he said with a grin.

Cindy laughed. Everyone in town referred to him as the town Jesus. Not in an irreverent way, just as a matter of fact. He had played Jesus for eight years in a row. Others had tried to copy him, but nobody could grow their hair and their beard the way he could. He enjoyed the attention he received from passersby on the street, but hated the "opposite" attention he got from the girls. It seemed no self-respecting girl wanted to have sex or even make out with Jesus. It really hurt his game.

Cindy began to ring up his products.

"Looks like it's going to be a big night at your house — conditioning your hair and scrubbing your toilet?"

Luke's face began to flush a little red. He wondered if that was a dig at his non-existent social life. Cindy sensed his embarrassment and tried to smooth everything over.

"Just teasing. Hey, speaking of conditioning your long Jesus-like hair, are you spoken for?"

Luke's heart jumped. He saw Cindy as being quite good-looking, with her long, thick hair and sexy brown eyes.

"No. I'm totally single," he answered hopefully.

"Oh Jesus, I mean God, I mean . . . I was talking about next year's parade."

She watched his handsome, regal face fall, and immediately felt full of guilt. *But, what can I do?* she thought. *I can't go to a horror movie and watch a slasher cut a girl's head off, while sharing a coke and making out with Jesus — no matter how hot he is. Can I?*

"The Junior League called yesterday," he replied, his tone somewhat blue. "But I haven't called them back, yet."

"Oh, well, I'm doing the float for the store next year. I would *love* it if you could be our Savior. You'll get ten percent off all your purchases for a year."

"Sure. I'll be your Savior."

She didn't know how profound that statement would be at the time.

Now here it was, the day before the parade. How time had flown! Cindy gathered up her sewing box and headed to Luke's house. The other two guys were meeting there, so they could all be fitted at the same time. She finished their robes fairly quickly, and they all headed out to the yard to finish their game of flip-cup. None of them questioned for a moment how the young people in their town could so effortlessly turn a religious event into one filled with beer and games.

Cindy was left with Luke. He took off his shirt, and she nearly fainted. His body was truly a work of God. She chuckled, as she thought of Gillian's response when she'd pleaded with her to do the fitting, so she could stay and supervise the float assembly.

"If I had to touch that man, I'd have to convert to Catholicism."

"Why's that?" Cindy asked.

"Because I'd be too embarrassed to ask the Big Guy to forgive me himself. Just something wrong with asking him to overlook the fact that you ravished a man that looks like his son."

111

"You're disgusting!" Cindy answered. However, she still wondered how she could argue with logic like that.

So, here she was. Trying to keep her mind on the task at hand—just measuring the hem, with a few safety pins inserted here and there. What she *wasn't* expecting was the fact that Luke was feeling really good about being pinned by her. So good that the measurement was near impossible to take, given that the next day, during the parade, the robe would be a good four or five inches longer in the front.

This is the time when Luke asked himself, *What would Jesus do?*

But, being human as he was, he did the only thing he felt he could do. He grabbed Cindy and kissed her. He kissed her long and hard on her soft lips. His long, conditioned hair mixed with hers, as he tasted the strawberry lip gloss she wore.

Cindy had never been kissed like that before. There had been the awkward kisses in middle school, when she feared her braces would lock with those worn by the boy she kissed. There had been one horrid kiss in high school, during which the tongue of the kissee seemed to move so fast inside her mouth, she began to feel nauseous. There were boring kisses, short pecks, nervous good night kisses . . . *none* had ever shot through her like Luke's kiss.

Moments seemed like hours, as he cradled her face with his soft hands. When he pulled away, she didn't know which way was up. She actually felt her knees buckle, and realized she had been standing on her tiptoes for more than five minutes.

"I'm sorry," Luke said. "I've just had the biggest crush on you ever since I can remember."

He looked slightly embarrassed, but also in total control. Cindy finally opened her eyes. She stared up at him in wonderment and thought, *I've been to the Promised Land, and I'm not leaving.*

Reaching up to caress his soft hair, she rose up on her toes again and pulled him toward her, aching for another kiss. Before long, the neatly pinned robe was on the floor and Cindy was in heaven, again and again. The only sounds were the howls of the flip-cup game and Cindy's whisper, "Oh God, Oh Jesus, you feel so good."

The next day, Cindy could barely contain herself, as she posed Luke on the front of the float. She pictured the two of them lying on a bed of tampons, making passionate love. It was everything she could do to stay focused on the task at hand. Cindy repeated, *Finish the float, win the prize money,* over and over in her head. She stayed composed enough to send the float down the roadway, and heard the cheering as it turned down Main Street. Now, all she could do was pray and wait.

13 TRUE LOVE ALL AROUND

I was emailin' back and forth with Drew the other day. Bein' in prison like he is, he gets lonely and bored. I usually don't share information about my clients with anyone, but I let him in on some of my cases. I don't reveal their names or nothin', but I think he likes hearin' about other people who are living life outside of prison. I told him all about Cindy and the parade. I also told him a little bit about her Jesus. He said he sure wished he could have seen it.

I feel like I've really found a friend in Drew, as strange as that may sound. It's real easy to tell him everything, knowin' that I ain't ever goin' to meet him or nothing. I tell him all about Wayne, too. He thinks that Wayne seems like a real nice man. "Quite a catch," he said. He told me if he were me, he'd hold onto him. He wrote, 'True love seems like it's just about impossible to find.'

Drew has only been in love one time. He said he had been sure he was going to get married and have kids, until he

114

found his girlfriend, Dee Ann, with another man. She'd had four kids, all by different daddies; but Drew didn't care. He still wanted to be with her, and take care of those kids as if they were his own. As far as he was concerned, they were real sweet kids and two of em' even called him Daddy.

Then, Dee Ann up and left him one day, out of the blue. Told him he was a sweet guy and all, but the daddy of her second baby had come over and asked her for another chance. She told Drew she had to choose, and she didn't choose him. I think it takes a big man to tell someone something like that, so I felt touched by him sharin' that with me.

I feel real bad about what he's going through now, though . . . and I'm prayin' extra hard for him.

14 GREETINGS FROM WARE STATE PRISON

Drew grabbed the envelope that was passed through the prison bars, along with a book he had requested entitled *Live Your Life as if it is Ending Tomorrow*. He rarely got mail. When he saw the return address, he smiled. His cousin, Charles, had only written him three times since he had been in prison. Usually, in his letters, Charles just bragged about his latest conquest. He was a ladies man, much like Drew. His last letter ended with: *I wouldn't want to be you, man. No breasts to rub, no thighs to caress, and no lips to kiss... unless you've had a change of heart and decided that Tom or Harry are looking pretty good to you. I'm hoping that's not the case, though, because when you get out of there, I'm taking you to the Paradise Gentleman's Club for a night of fun. Hang in there.*

Charles was Drew's mother's sister's son. They had grown up in towns only a few hours apart, so they often saw each other on holidays and during the summer months. When they'd grown up, Charles visited Drew many times in Atlanta, and they always had fun together. The big city always had the right mix of drinking and ladies for both of them.

Drew opened the letter and sat on his cot. It read:

Hey Drew,

I'm writing with a great business opportunity. I was recently fired from my job. I took my severance pay and headed down to the Dominican Republic for some R&R. I had to get out of town for a while and regroup. I was hanging out at the casino in Puerto Playa having a beer, and I met this man who moved down here fourteen years ago. He was a real interesting guy. Anyway, he told me he's planning on moving back to New York in a few months, because his daughter is about to have her first baby. He wants to leave paradise to be with a snotty-nosed kid. Anyway, he started this beach equipment rental business, and he's looking to sell it. They rent kayaks, sailboards, floats and things like that. He's willing to sell for $25,000. There's a little beach shack, not far from there, that we could stay in until we make enough money to get our own places. He says he clears about $800 a week. It wouldn't take too long. What do you think? His daughter is due in seven months, and you'll be out by then. Can you come up with $12,500 to move to paradise? Let me know what you think. You and me, two bottles of cold beer, *and tanned tourists in their bikinis . . . how can you resist?*

Your Cuz

Drew closed his eyes and thought about the offer. It's not like he had anything else lined up. Hell, he didn't even have anywhere else to go. Amanda's husband, the judge, had come to his hearing and told him that if he ever set foot in Atlanta again, he would make sure that his life was a living hell. The judge said he would hunt him down like a buck during hunting season. So, relocating to a Caribbean island sounded like a good alternative to being hunted down. The money was the problem. *Where can I come up with that kind of cash in just a few months?* Drew wondered. Having only about $2,000 in the bank, he needed a plan . . . and fast. That's when the idea hit him. If he was smart about it, and really used his charm, he could pull it off.

He quickly scribbled a note back to Charles. *"I'm in,"* it read. *"See you in paradise!"*

15 CHASTITY AGREEMENT... SIGN ON THE DOTTED LINE

Wayne and I are like two peas in a pod. We do just about everything together. Well, almost everything. That's where things are getting a little tricky, right about now. We've been together six weeks and two days. Most men wouldn't have been as patient as Wayne has been about . . . well, you know, having sex. Of course, I vowed many years ago, back in my tenth grade Sunday school class, that I would wait 'til I was married. I even signed a chastity agreement. Back then, it wasn't such a hard thing to ask. To tell you the truth, I was happy to sign it. I didn't have much interest in doin' it at all.

Now, I'm struggling. I know Wayne is the one for me, and I know God sent him to me, and I know he is a man with needs. I'm just questionin' whether or not that means I can meet those needs before we get married. Wayne's gotten pretty heavy with the kissin' and makin' out. I'm not

119

complaining, either. He knows what to do to make me feel good. The other night, I wadn't so sure I was going to be able to stop myself. I guess the good Lord was looking out for me and leadin' me away from temptation, because just as my jeans was gettin' unbuttoned, my phone rang. It was one of the residents of the trailer park. There was a stray dog wanderin' around her trailer and he was gettin' into her garbage cans.

I buttoned my jeans back up and told Wayne I was gonna' have to go and see about the situation.

"Come on, babe. Now? Can't it wait til' tomorrow? I've got a situation that needs tendin' to, as well."

I kissed him on the forehead and told him I was sorry. As I walked to see about the dog, I was thinkin' about Peggy Rogers. She was the one who suggested we have our chastity agreement. If I remember right, I think she is even the one who wrote it. It was written on fancy paper, decorated with little swirls around the corners. At the time, she was datin' Mark Schultz, the senior class president and the quarterback of the football team. He was in our Sunday school class, too. We all signed our names on the dotted lines, vowin' to save the secret gift that God gave to us, until we were bonded in marriage.

Peggy seemed real proud she had influenced us all in such a good way. That was until Mark Schultz was caught with Mandy. Yes, Mandy who is now the head of the quiltin' group. Back then, she was head of the Pep Club. Their job was to make sure the athletes were all excited and pumped up before a game. Mandy did a real good job of gettin' Mark pumped up. The coach caught them in the locker room shower, buck naked before a game. It didn't take long for word to get out around the school about the two of them, since the rest of the team filed in soon after the coach. They all got an eyeful.

Mandy showed up at Sunday School the next week with her parents, who blamed themselves for not makin' sure she was in church more often. They weren't real good about gettin' to church. Things didn't sit well in that particular class, seein' as how Peggy, Mark and Mandy were all sittin' around the same table.

The chastity agreement that had been signed earlier was hangin' on the wall as a reminder to us all. When we got to class the first day after the shower incident, Mark's name was crossed out in black marker. Beside it was written the word "sinner." Peggy glared at them both, throughout the whole class.

After gettin' word about what happened through town gossip, the teacher taught a real nice lesson, though . . . on Colossians 3:13: "Bear with each other and forgive whatever grievances you may have against one another. Forgive as the Lord forgave you."

I thought that when the lesson was over, they would move past this big ol' mess; but it didn't happen. They walked out of class and into the fellowship hall, where the congregation always had doughnuts and coffee before the church service. Mark grabbed three doughnuts and went to sit by himself over in the corner of the room. I noticed that Peggy was dabbin' her eyes with her napkin, as she watched him shove the doughnuts into his mouth. Mandy was standin' by the exit, looking a little lost. She looked over at Peggy and then at Mark. I swear Mandy actually smiled, unbuttoned the top button on her sweater, poked her chest out some and fluffed her hair. Then, she grabbed a carton of milk and walked over to Mark. Mandy bent down to set it on the table in front of him. When she did, even I, across the room, could see the voluptuous gifts God had blessed her with.

That was enough to send Peggy into a tailspin. She flew across the room, grabbed the milk and dumped it on Mandy's head. In response, Mandy turned around real fast, and I thought she was going to slap her. Instead, she took a deep breath, broke out in tears, and fell to the floor, crying out, "Peggy, why are you doing this to me? I just want forgiveness from you and from God. Please, won't you forgive me?"

Peggy just stood there. Everyone was looking, including Reverend Sanders and all those who had gone to Sunday school that morning. Peggy ran out the door, and Mandy just sat on the floor crying. It was quite a scene. The little old ladies from the Seniors Only Class hurried over to Mandy and rushed her into the bathroom.

After that, Peggy started going to the Methodist Church and Mandy became the pet of the senior class. They are the ones who told her God would always forgive her, and they taught her, within just a few weeks' time, how to quilt. She found her place in the church. Now, nobody even seems to remember what ever happened. The chastity agreement disappeared from the wall, apparently along with the group's memory of all of Mandy's transgressions.

I wondered if my transgressions with Wayne would be wiped from everyone's memories, should they find out. Wayne had waited so long, and I knew he wouldn't wait too much longer before he thought about fulfilling his needs somewhere else. I prayed for God to show me what to do. Then, I went to chase off that stray dog.

16 FRANKIE'S INVITATION

Frankie opened the front door and made her way to the mailbox. The weather was warm and balmy. *The Fourth of July will be here before I know it*, she thought, reflecting back to the first July Fourth she and Ed had celebrated together in the Hamptons. They had thrown such a lovely party. They had Maine lobster, Idaho potatoes, Texas sheet cake and Kentucky mint juleps. There had been more states represented, but it was so long ago, Frankie couldn't remember which ones they were. The fireworks over the water had been spectacular, though—she recalled that clearly.

As she pulled the mail from the mailbox, Frankie smiled at the memory of Ed kissing her, while gentle waves washed over their feet and the sky twinkled with starlight and fireworks in the distance. It was like a scene in a movie. You couldn't have staged it any better.

She shuffled through the mail, only to find the usual: credit card applications, the grocery store circular- . . . *Wait!* she thought. *What's this?* She held in her right hand a beautifully addressed envelope. Five by seven . . . standard invitation size, but obviously an important occasion, because the letter size dictated more postage than usual. Frankie ripped the envelope open and her breath caught.

Please join us to celebrate the homecoming of our son.
Saturday, November 18th
At 4:00 pm
RSVP to Marcia

Frankie was surprised. Marcia had lived in the house next door for many years before Frankie and Ed had purchased their home. She had given Frankie a beautiful orchid when they moved into the house. And only one week later, she had sent a lovely funeral arrangement with a thoughtful card to Frankie, urging her to call if she needed anything. Frankie could barely bring herself to talk to people who she had known for years during this time, much less make idle chit-chat with a complete stranger. She sent the obligatory thank-you card and always smiled and waved when they crossed paths taking the garbage out or getting the mail. However, that was the extent of their acquaintance.

She scratched her head in puzzlement. As she walked back to the house, Frankie debated the pros and cons of the party. Of course, on the pro list . . . it was a party. *Oh, how long has it been!* she thought. Cons: well, she hadn't been to a party in five years, with the exception of Ed's wake, which she walked through in a Prozac-induced stupor. Her heart fluttered at the thought of music and people chatting happily. Feeling carefree and happy in the moment, Frankie speculated that maybe this was her prayers being answered. Well, not only her prayers, but the prayers of the Prayer Lady. *She must have some pull,* Frankie concluded. Even if she didn't, Frankie just felt a special need to send money to a soul so devout, that she spent every day praying for others.

Back to the party, she thought. *It's been so long. I'll need to take a thank-you gift and maybe something for their son.* She wondered where he had been. Frankie searched her mind for any inkling of their son. She realized she didn't even know they had a son. *Maybe he's in the military,* she thought. *Shipped off to the Middle East, maybe? It might be nice to get out.* She decided to sleep on it.

That night, as she drifted into her dreams, she clutched to the hope that Ed would visit her. Instead, Grams crept into her dreams. She was by a long pool, drenched in moonlight. Her hair was bobbed, and she held a long cigarette between her fingers. She saw herself walk toward Grams. Frankie was dressed in her bathrobe—the one she spent most of her days in. Her hair was a mess from the last quick trip she'd made to Great Clips. It was almost totally gray, now that she hadn't had it colored in five years. As she reached out to hug Grams, Grams pushed her away.

"I declare, Frankie, you look dreadful! You might as well just go ahead and put the other foot in the grave. You've taken all the fun out of living. All that I taught you is gone. You know who I see when I look at you,

Duckie? Your mother, bless her soul. She just didn't know what living was all about. Never thought I would see you that way! I thought you had more of me in you, but I guess not."

Suddenly, one of Gram's favorite songs began playing on a victrola. She jumped up and down and started clapping. They're playin' my song!"

She began to disappear.

"Wait," Frankie tried to shout, but nothing would come out of her mouth.

She woke feeling deflated and sad, then got out of bed and made a cup of hot milk. Frankie laughed as she thought about Grams—the grandmother who always had a smile and a cup of hooch. Dumping her milk into the sink, she walked to Ed's liquor cabinet and poured a big jigger full of Johnny Walker. She raised the glass tumbler in her hand and toasted the air.

"Here's to you, Grams!" She guzzled the drink and shook her head, as the burn made its way down her throat. Frankie glanced at the clock. Seeing it was 3:47, she decided there was time to sleep later. She pulled out a notepad and a pen. There was a lot to do before the party next week. She began her to-do list with, "RSVP *yes* to Marcia."

Frankie made an appointment at Les Cheveux Fabuleux for Thursday. Her first call had left her feeling rejected. *Of course*, there was no way they could fit her in for at least six weeks. But Frankie called back and pulled on her old powers of persuasion, securing an appointment three days away . . . *with the owner*, no less. Leo would stay after hours, just for her. Of course, Frankie's offer of $1,000 dollars went a long way in persuading the establishment to help her. Something about the thought of a new haircut hit her. It was the start to a new Frankie.

As Frankie walked away from Leo and exited the salon — with stylish light brown and blonde highlighted hair, which framed her face perfectly — she felt lighter, somehow. She and Leo had quickly become best friends. She smiled inside, knowing she still had that Frankie charm, which she hadn't used in years. For the first time in quite a while, she remembered how good it was to have a friend.

Number two on her to-do list was . . . *find something to wear.* The next item down the list called to her, though; she had to stop by the grocery store to pick up coffee, knowing she couldn't function without a cup first thing in the morning. Upon arriving at the store, she grabbed her coffee and decided to have a salmon for dinner. Frankie also picked up a bottle of wine, somehow feeling alive for the first time in years. As she waited at the check-out counter, she picked up a *Cosmopolitan* magazine and thumbed through it for ideas on what to wear to the party. As she flipped the pages, she stopped on an article titled, "Hand & Mouth... not just a toddler virus." She laughed at the cleverness of the writer. Another customer walked to the cashier and politely tapped her on the shoulder.

"Excuse me, I'm looking for guava jelly and persimmons?" she asked.

"Let me page our manager for you," the cashier answered.

Frankie watched as a gawky-looking man walked toward the woman. As he approached, the woman acted as though she was seeing Brad Pitt.

"Oh. Hi, Arnold. I'm so glad to see you. I mean, I'm looking for guava jelly? Oh, uh, and persimmons."

Frankie watched with curiosity. She remembered days in Studio 54 when code was used frequently. This had to be code. *That woman phrased her comment like a question*, she noticed. Frankie eyed them suspiciously. She had seen what drugs had done to her friends at Studio 54. After she'd married Ed, she continually heard about friends who had OD'd. Something tugged at her. Somehow, Frankie immediately felt she needed to find out what was happening. She put the *Cosmo* magazine back in its place and looked into her basket.

"Oh, my goodness, I forgot my guava jelly and persimmons."

The cashier winked at her and nodded toward the back right hand corner of the store. She leaned over to Johnnie and whispered in her ear, "It's the door marked 'Storeroom.'"

Johnnie walked toward the back of the store and played scenarios in her head. What was she really going to do? She had enjoyed everything that this poor housewife had enjoyed. Back in the day, there wasn't a drug that evaded her. She was lucky she had found a way out, before she ended up in some stranger's bed without a pulse.

Frankie pushed open the storeroom door with a resolve to save whomever was about to make a deal with "the Devil," that manager Arnold. When she finished saving the pitiful housewife, she was going to give Arnold a piece of her mind. Frankie decided she might even have to call the police. Grams would be disappointed, but crack was a lot different than prohibited hooch.

As the door slammed open, the housewife and Arnold jumped. Arnold quickly pushed the door closed and sized up Frankie.

"Are you looking for guava jelly and persimmons?" he asked.

She looked around for the shot needles, the mirrored lines of coke or a smoking bong. Then she faced Arnold with a confused look.

"I'm not sure? What exactly is guava jelly and persimmons?"

Arnold cleared his throat, and the housewife looked as though she would run out the door at any minute.

"I'm Arnold, the manager here at Shop and Save. May I ask you why you asked for guava jelly and persimmons?"

"I just heard this lady ask for them and got worried. Are you dealing in here?" She glared at his nametag. "Arnold?"

A look registered on Arnold's face . . . a look of relief. As he briefly stared at Frankie, her easy going nature put him at ease. He knew immediately he had a friend in Frankie.

"No, ma'am. I can assure you there are no drugs in this room. Quite the contrary, I am selling couture that is available to my clients without the knowledge of their husbands. "

Frankie stared at him with a puzzled look on her face.

"What do you mean?"

"Simply put, you can purchase couture clothing here in the storeroom. Your credit card bill will read simply 'Shop & Save.'"

He stood a little taller and continued, "The price of groceries have grown quite a bit over the last few years. The potato farmers have gone on strike. Organic foods are a lot more expensive than traditionally grown produce. The freeze here in Florida has even made the price of orange juice skyrocket. Grocery bills are getting larger and larger in my store."

A light bulb went off in Frankie's head. She looked around in astonishment.

"You might be the most ingenious man I've met since my husband," she said.

"I don't know about ingenious, but definitely lucky to have such good customers," he said, winking at the housewife. "Let me just finish ringing up this purchase, and I'll give you the tour."

Frankie laughed at herself. She had just jumped from a long dark stupor into paranoia into luck. She really needed something for the party she was going to attend. The *InStyle Magazine* was so full of fashion that she didn't know which way to turn. Maybe Arnold could save her the embarrassment of walking through the mall without the slightest idea as to what a fashionable woman her age should wear. The housewife grabbed her bag and gave Arnold a quick kiss on the cheek. She then turned to Frankie and gave her a wink and a smile.

"Happy shopping!" she said, before heading out of the storeroom.

Frankie waved and then turned her attention to Arnold. He noticed she still seemed a little nervous, so he tried to put her at ease.

"I know I've seen you in the store before, occasionally, but I've never learned your name," he said, sticking out his hand. Frankie reached forward and clutched his hand with heartfelt happiness.

"You can call me Frankie. I'm really sorry about my previous suspicions."

"Don't think twice about it. I think you are very brave for bounding through the door the way you did."

"I would call myself anything but brave, Arnold."

Frankie looked down at her feet. She could feel the tears welling. It had been a long time since she had cried. It had been a long time since she had laughed. *God, where have the last five years gone*, she thought.

Arnold had gained quite a bit of composure over the past few months. The women in the store seemed to genuinely like and appreciate what he was offering. But he felt totally incapable of dealing with a crying woman. His mother had never shed a tear in his presence. Other than her, he had no real experience dealing with women, except for their excitement over a new purse or their nervousness as they made their first purchase in the storeroom. They had come to trust his fashion sense, which was becoming quite keen, as he daily perused the fashion websites and magazines that came through the store.

He quickly wondered what in the world to do. As he frantically pondered his options, Frankie's crying came on even harder. She walked to the side of the room and turned her head in embarrassment. Arnold felt sorry for the lady, but the tears were beginning to fall on the season's most coveted Coach purse. He decided he had to act quickly. Pulling his handkerchief from his pocket, he handed it to her. Then, he pulled a chair from the corner of the room and gently guided her to it.

"I tell you what...stay here for a minute, and I'll be right back."

Frankie continued to sob but managed a nod.

Arnold remembered Chuck telling him about his escapades. "Wine," he'd told him, "is the key to a woman. Give her wine, and you'll know her."

Arnold had met plenty of women at the Shop and Save, and thus far, hadn't needed wine. But with a woman on the verge of a nervous breakdown in the store room, he didn't know what else to do. Grabbing a bottle of Merlot — with a twist-top — from the wine aisle, he quickly purchased it through the self-checkout. Unlike Chuck, Arnold didn't want to take anything that wasn't his. He needed to be as clean as a whistle to avoid the attention of corporate. He made his way to the water cooler in the employees' lounge. After grabbing a paper cup from the water dispenser, he poured a glass, took a deep breath and walked back into the storeroom.

"Here you go, Frankie. You look like you could use this."

Frankie took the cup and drained its contents. "I'm so sorry, Arnold. This isn't me . . . I promise." She held out the cup for Arnold to refill.

"I've been in Jacksonville for five years, Arnold. I've probably only been out of my home a couple of dozen times. I thought life was over for me."

Arnold was at a loss of words. He had no clue what to say next. So he just smiled and nodded his head at Frankie. He took a guzzle from the wine bottle, hoping it would calm his nerves.

Frankie's tears continued for three hours and through another bottle of wine. She told Arnold all about Studio54, the baby, and Ed's heart attack. She told him about the last five years, too, but that only took five minutes.

A clerk tapped on the door. "Come in," Arnold said.

A forty-something, bleached blond cashier stood in the doorway. "Sorry to bother you, sir, but the customers have cleared out. I'm cashed out and ready to head home. Do you need anything else?"

"No, thank you, Martha, that'll be it. If you'll just turn off the main lights and lock the door, I would appreciate it. Do you want me to walk you to your car?"

"No. My boyfriend is waiting for me in the parking lot."

"Okay, have a good night. See you tomorrow?"

"Yes, I'll be in at 2:00," she answered.

"Alright, good-bye."

Arnold looked back at Frankie. She was smiling now. *When you smile*, he thought, *you look much younger.* He wondered if he should tell her so. He liked Frankie. She had lived her life, when he had hidden from his. Now, the tables were turned. She had been hiding, when he had finally gotten up the nerve to live — glasses, acne and all.

"Do you believe in fate, Arnold?" Frankie asked.

"I don't know. If fate made me an outcast in school, gave me no friends, and forced me to live with my mother until I was twenty-five-then no. I don't want to believe in fate."

Frankie pondered his answer. Somewhere in the back of her mind, she heard her grandmother's voice.

Frankie narrowed in on the memory and saw herself walking into Grams' house. She and her mother had had another fight. Frankie stormed into Grams's living room and threw her palms up into the air. "I guess it's just my fate to have a mother who hates me!"

Grams looked up from her book and laughed. "You're a modern woman, Frankie. Modern women make their own fate!"

It hit Frankie like a lightning bolt. *How stupid I've been,* she thought. *I thought fate took my baby and Ed from me. I thought that fate turned me from a party queen into a hermit for five years. That wasn't fate,* she thought. *That was my own self-pity.*

She wasn't supposed to be this woman. She *could* be the Frankie who'd made out with Rocky and partied with Liza. The woman who'd had the New York elite by the earlobe. She was Frankie, damn it!

"By God, Arnold. I think you may be my savior!"

Arnold laughed at the proclamation. She finished her cup of wine and stood up.

"Enough of this pity-party. You have to help me find an outfit for an upcoming event. I want to look so good that I knock the socks off everyone there! Hey, *why don't you come with me?* We'll really give them something to talk about!"

"Frankie, I haven't really been to many parties."

"Oh, don't be silly. *Everyone* goes to parties. Surely there was a big party after your senior prom?"

Arnold shook his head slowly. "There was a party, but I didn't go because I didn't go to prom."

"Okay, what about a wedding reception. Those are always fun. Maybe a friend or cousin got married and you danced the night away to awful line dances?"

Again, Arnold shook his head no.

"I'm sure you've at least been to a birthday party?"

Arnold eyebrows shot up. "Actually, I *have* been to a birthday party. Martha, the cashier who came in earlier, had a birthday party for her daughter when she turned three. I went to that party!"

Frankie rolled her eyes. "Dear Lord, Arnold, looks like there might be such a thing as fate. You need me as much as I need you! Okay, here's the deal—you help me find an amazing outfit to wear to the coming home party . . . and I'll show you how much fun a *real* party can be."

Arnold agreed without a moment's hesitation. Frankie jotted down her address and added the date and time of the party beneath it. Immediately, he began pulling out a beautiful pink silk top adorned with red hibiscus flowers. He pictured Frankie with white linen pants and red strappy sandals. While getting an outfit assembled for Frankie, Arnold was almost as excited to see her in it as he was to attend the party.

Frankie and Arnold became fast friends. Arnold had helped with Frankie's transformation, so Frankie figured the least she could do was help him with his— and it was easy to see how much he needed the help. She didn't know many people who wore glasses that thick. But she decided that contacts would be the best place to start. She was a little nervous about approaching him with her plan, not wanting to offend him and risk losing her best and only friend.

Frankie coaxed him into going to lunch with her on the following Monday. The store was generally slow on Mondays, so it didn't take much urging. After polishing off a bowl of gazpacho and a salad, she broached the subject.

"Hey, Arnold, have you ever thought about wearing contacts?" She reached over and pulled the glasses from his face. He immediately scrunched his face up, trying to bring his surroundings into focus. After a few seconds with no luck, he stared at approximately where Frankie was sitting. His mother had always warned him against wearing contacts.

"They'll trap all kinds of dirt and germs right against your eyeball," she'd say. "Is that what you want? You'll probably end up blind. Would you rather be a little more appealing to the girls and blind as a bat? I think not." With that, she would stomp off to the kitchen.

He had heard the same argument for so many years, that he just put the thought of contacts right out of his mind. But now that he had a good job and his own apartment, Arnold decided, right then and there, he might as well stretch his independence even more.

Frankie had been one step ahead of him. She had scheduled an appointment with Dr. Lasher a few weeks before. By 4:27 that very day, Arnold emerged from the office with beautiful green eyes and a bottle of saline solution. Frankie gasped when he came out from the office and smiled at her.

"You look wonderful! Ready for stop number two?"

Arnold glanced at his watch. "Oh, Frankie, I need to get back to the store. Vaughn gets off in thirty minutes."

"Vaughn is just fine. I spoke to her yesterday. She is going to close up for you."

She laced her arm through his and led him to the car. They pulled into Les Cheveux Fabuleux's parking lot. The owner was more than happy to see Frankie's friend. The amount of her last tip was still dancing in his head. But as Arnold and Frankie walked in, money wasn't the only thing holding his attention.

"Frankie, who is this and where have you been hiding him?"

Frankie proudly thrust Arnold into a nearby salon chair. "This is my dearest friend in the whole world, Arnold."

"Well, dearest friend Arnold, it's a good thing you're here. Don't worry about this mess here," he said, as he ran his fingers through Arnold's hair. "I hope you are suing!"

Arnold stared at him blankly.

"Suing the butcher who ravaged your hair! It's *atrocious*."

Arnold managed a chuckle and a nod, before picturing himself a few weeks earlier, sitting on a stool in his mother's kitchen with chunks of hair falling onto her gold linoleum floor.

Leo turned to Frankie. "Sweetheart, why don't you pour us a glass of wine. It's in the fridge right around the corner. This is going to take some time."

Two bottles of wine and three cartons of Chinese take-out later, Arnold didn't even recognize himself. As he stared into the mirror, he saw a man who he didn't know existed. Truly, he doubted his own mother would even recognize him.

Frankie broke his trance, as she held up a *People* magazine. "These shoes are to die for," she said, pointing to a picture of a young starlet standing on a red carpet.

"Fender McCoys" both Arnold and Leo said at the same time. Leo's mouth dropped open in surprise. "He's handsome and knows his shoes, too? Frankie, you better get him out of here quick, before I steal your dearest friend and lock him up in my bedroom."

Arnold stood up and brushed the small hairs from his shoulders. He reached his hand out to shake Leo's hand, only to be clutched in a bear hug.

17 PEEPING EARL

I just love the holiday season. Christmas seems like it just fills up the air with joy! Reverend Sanders asked me if I would be in charge of the Stockings for the Poor this year. We ask all the Sunday school classes, the men's group, the choir, and just about any other group in our church to collect candy and little treats for the stockings. We stuff them and pass em' out to some of the children in our town who ain't got much. For a few, these stockings is all they get for Christmas.

I was real flattered when Reverend Sanders asked me to be in charge. Mrs. Whipple and a few of the other real active ladies in the church met me in the fellowship hall to get the goodies divided out and put in the stockings. On my way into the church, I was met at the door by Earl, the church janitor. Now, from the looks of Earl, you can pretty much tell that if he were a few years younger, he would be gettin' one of our stockings. He don't have much money, which makes you want to feel sorry for him. But, forgive me Lord, he gives me the creeps. He always has. Pretty much, Earl just kind of shuffles around the church, sweepin' here, pickin' up an old can there, and all the while kinda' watchin' you from behind his glasses — the kind that make his eyes look about five times bigger than they are. His hair is greasy, and he don't really talk. He just lurks.

Well, when I near about ran into him walkin' into the church, I almost jumped out of my skin! He gave me one of his creepy head nods and moved to the side, so I could get through the door. I hoped he wadn't going to pick this time to start cleanin' the fellowship hall where we were going to stuff the stockings. I didn't think I could take his lurking around while we were working. About that time, Mrs. Whipple rolled in along with a few of her friends. Luckily, they seemed to scare Earl right on out of there.

We had a ton of things for the kids. We stuffed forty-eight stockings 'til they were overflowing. Next, we had to divide them into boxes, so the men could deliver them to the children's houses. I sat there loading boxes with stuffed stockings, feelin' pretty darn good about what all of us were doin'. I guess you could say I could see clear through to the end, when all those little kids would wake up on Christmas morning and start pullin' candy and toys out of these very stockings. Who wouldn't want to be part o' that?

Well, after filling up one box after another and talkin' with the ladies for awhile, I excused myself, so I could go to the bathroom. I was about to wet my pants, after all the sweet tea I'd drunk. Once inside the ladies room, as I sat down and began to pee, I heard a sound above my head. I looked up and there was a vent right above my stall. That wadn't too out of the ordinary, by itself; but what was, was the big old coke bottle eyes that was starin' at me through the vent. I just froze mid-stream. I didn't know whether to

140

finish, wipe or scream. There we sat for about ten seconds, my big eyes starin' at his big eyes.

I decided to play it as cool as I could, until I could figure out what to do. I pulled my shirt down over my knees to cover any private part that might be showing, and I carefully stood and pulled up my pants.

I quickly went out of the bathroom and ran into Reverend Sander's office. I told him what had happened. He asked me if I was sure that I wadn't mistakin'. After I assured him, he went over to a closet that had stairs leadin' up to the attic space above the fellowship hall. He bolted that door closed from the outside.

"What are you going to do?" I asked him.

"I reckon I'm going to lock him in there, until the police get here," he said as he instructed Patty to call 911. I was shakin' up by all this, but knew that the ladies helpin' with the stockings weren't going to hang around much longer. So, I went back into the fellowship hall to finish up. They had the stockings divided up into neighborhoods, so they could be properly boxed and easily delivered.

We were just labelin' the boxes, when I heard some footsteps from somewhere overhead. Suddenly, as we all looked around for the source of the sound, Earl came crashin' through the ceiling. He fell right through the paneling and landed in the middle of the stockings! Candy canes and Christmas pencils went scatterin' everywhere. Earl's glasses were crooked on his face and plaster was crumbled all over his clothes.

Reverend Sanders came runnin' in with Dan, the deputy sheriff, right on his heels. Lucky for us, Dan had been just around the corner at the barbershop and had come quickly when he got the 911 call.

He took one look at Earl and shook his head. "Earl, you have the right to remain silent." Grabbing his arm, he pulled him off our stockings and up onto his feet. Dan looked around at the church ladies, who were all too scared to move. "It's okay, everyone. Earl won't be bothering you again."

Earl looked around with the same expression he always wore. Didn't seem he even knew what had happened. I guess he didn't know that the attic floor wadn't finished out. Seems he panicked when Reverend Sanders locked the door and pretty quick, just took off runnin' around up there, like some kind of trapped animal.

Dan told us Earl had been caught peepin' in windows when he was a teenager. After havin' to go through some sort of teen counseling program, they thought he was rehabilitated. Instead, he was gettin' his kicks by peepin' at good church-going ladies when they were in the bathroom! I usually have a pretty good sense about people, especially concernin' whether or not they're good or bad. I knew there was something off about ol' Earl.

Even though I think what he did is disgusting, I'll add him to my personal prayer list, for a while, anyway.

18 THE COMING HOME PARTY COMES AROUND

As Johnny packed his bag, the pain shot through his back every time he bent over to pick up a shirt or a pair of underwear. He pushed through the darts of discomfort and wondered how long it would last—that is, whether every day of his life would be filled with the throbbing he now felt. As if the question was being broadcast to the universe, Trent walked in with the answer.

"Hey, buddy, still feeling like shit? Not to worry, I asked a bone reader in Jackson Square about my best friend, and he said, 'Your friend will soon find happiness and the love of his life.' He's been on Jackson Square since before Katrina. He knows what he's talking about. No doubt."

Johnny smiled at his friend's impeccable timing. Trenton took one look at Johnny's suitcase and began to shake his head. "Come on, man, don't you even know how to fold a shirt?" He motioned towards the chair by the windows. "Sit down and let me help you out." He began refolding the shirts and pants. Creases were pressed and wrinkles were smoothed. After the suitcase was securely fastened, Trenton sat on the foot of the bed, facing Johnny. "I have some news for you. The voodoo lady contacted me back. She said you need to go back to Florida. She said that's where your lady awaits."

Johnny smiled. He had to laugh at the fervor with which Trenton approached his 'lady,'" as Trenton called her.

"Well, it's a good thing that's where I'm heading."

"Yes it is, isn't it. I'm happy to be driving you back to where your destiny awaits. Now, get off your ass and let's get moving. I'm sick of the smell of this place! Four weeks is enough time for anyone to get themselves outta' here."

The nurse wheeled in a wheelchair and Trent rolled his eyes. "For God's sake, he's not an invalid!"

The nurse stared at Trenton. "It's hospital policy, sir."

"Damn, does that mean I have to carry this suitcase all the way to the fifth floor of the parking garage?"

The nurse merely smiled.

As the nurse whisked Johnny by Trenton, Trenton rolled his eyes and chuckled. "You owe me, buddy."

As the journey home began, Johnny drifted in and out of sleep. Trenton spoke non-stop when Johnny was alert, but listened to the radio and sang quietly when

144

he slept. Looking over at him periodically as he slept, Trenton wanted to check to be sure his chest was moving. The accident had shaken him up more than he'd let on. He considered Johnny his one true friend. Of course, lots of people were his *friends*. With his 'larger than life' personality and the easygoing way he moved through life, Trenton knew many people who would consider themselves his friends. But Johnny was the only one who he felt he could confide in.

In fact, he had been planning on confiding in him on the trip to New Orleans. He wondered if Johnny had taken notice of the fact that he hadn't been on a date with a woman for nearly two years. But, that would have to wait. Johnny needed him now, and he would be there for him- as he knew Johnny would be for him.

When they were a few miles from Johnny's house, Trenton gave him a little nudge on the knee.

"Hey, wake up, Johnny. This has been the most boring road trip of all times! Not only do you make me drive the whole way, you don't even bother to keep me company."

Johnny opened his eyes, looked out the window, and immediately recognized the lush greenery of his home town. "Sorry, man. I'm so used to sleeping away the days in the hospital."

"It's okay. You'll get your groove back. You just need some time on the beach with the breeze blowing across your face."

***

As Arnold followed the MapQuest directions to Frankie's house, he began to get nervous. Frankie was such a nice woman when they were together. They had enjoyed numerous in-store fashion shows, during which she'd try on outfit after outfit. Once they found the perfect one, they'd celebrate by lunching at Bistro 54, a fancy restaurant that had just opened. Afterwards, they'd visit the posh boutiques lining the streets along the fashion district. Arnold had already surmised Frankie was not hurting for money; but as he drove down the wealthiest street in town, he realized he may have underestimated her worth.

Pulling into her driveway, Arnold gasped. His newfound friend lived in a *mansion*. Exotic palm trees lined the long driveway, which was beautifully adorned with hibiscuses and other tropical flowers. Before him stood a classic Mediterranean house, trimmed out handsomely with elegant ironwork. The house sprawled across a lush green yard. He stopped in the circular drive, which featured a large, white marble fountain gently splashing alongside of it.

Arnold paused, realizing he might not be properly dressed. He had spent so much time learning about women's fashion, it felt second nature to him, now. However, he didn't feel as confident about men's fashion. Arnold had decided on a pair of khaki slacks and a breezy white cotton shirt. It was casual, yet polished. Or so he had thought, when he'd dressed earlier that day. *Now*, he wondered if he looked like he should be serving fruity drinks at a tropical poolside resort bar.

He only had seconds to ponder the thought before Frankie came bounding out of the door. "Oh, Arnold, don't you just look wonderful!" She grabbed his hand and pulled him into the most magnificent foyer he had ever seen . . . *anywhere* (that is, even on TV or in a magazine!).

Frankie led him through the foyer and into a kitchen that would suit *any* famous chef. She had a bottle of white wine chilling in a silver bucket on the dappled grey marble island. There were also two crystal wine glasses on the countertop and a tray of assorted cheeses adorned with fruit and fancy looking crackers.

"I figured we could have a little party *of our own* before we head next door. What do you think?"

"Sure, Frankie. Listen, I was wondering if I'm underdressed?"

"Don't be silly, darling! It's not *what* you wear, but *how* you wear it. You just walk right into that party as if you've always known everyone there and as if you feel right at home in the space. That puts everyone you come across at ease. You'll be the toast of the party."

"Frankie, you're too good to me. You're really the only friend I've ever had, you know."

Frankie squeezed his hand. "You are a good friend, too, Arnold. I was lost when I found you. Now, I feel like living again. I feel like I'm back. We're good for each other, you and I. We'll be friends for a long time. I can just feel it."

She poured them both a glass of wine. "Grab your drink and come with me. I'll show you the rest of the house."

Fifteen minutes later, after their tour of the house was finished, Arnold felt slightly dizzy. *Her place*, he thought, *is so huge and so stunning*. He remembered Frankie as he first met her in the store. He knew she hadn't gotten out of the house much since her husband died- and that had been many years ago. She had seemed so lonely and fragile. Now, she was strong and vibrant. He was glad their paths had crossed.

"Arnold, did you hear me?" Frankie asked.

"I'm sorry, what did you say?"

"I was saying we should have a party—you and I. We just have to think of an occasion or theme, and then put together a guest list. That's a little hard for me, since the only people I know in this town are our new hairdresser and the sweet staff at your store."

"Well, I don't really have many friends either, Frankie. The only people I see on a regular basis are my customers."

"That's it! We'll have a Shop & Save special trunk show, right here in my home! Oh, Arnold, it'll be *fabulous*. We can display things throughout the house. I'll set up dressing rooms at different locations, with full-length mirrors all around. We'll call it *'Shop & Save, then Wine & Dine!'*"

Frankie began clapping her hands, and was smiling from ear to ear.

"Sounds great, Frankie. Are you sure you're up to it?"

"Darling, I've never been more ready for anything in my life! We'll start the planning tomorrow morning. Let me sleep on it. I get many of my best ideas when I first wake up in the mornings. There's no telling what will be dancing around in this head when I wake up tomorrow."

She glanced up at the clock. "Goodness, we better get next door! Fashionably late is wonderful, but over thirty minutes late is just rude, in my book!"

As they walked down the front steps and across the lush manicured yard, Frankie gave Arnold a playful smile. "Maybe we'll find you a pretty girl at this shindig."

Arnold shook his head. "I wouldn't hold my breath, Frankie. My last date in eleventh grade was the worst night of my life. I think I could go through life just fine without ever putting another girl through a date with me."

"Eleventh grade? Arnold, you're really lucky you met me!" She laughed.

As he saw the up-to-no-good look in her eyes, Arnold got a little nervous.

They walked into Marcia and Lou's backyard, which was superbly landscaped and right on the St. John's River. The yard, like Frankie's, was shaded by giant oak trees, all of which were dripping with Spanish moss. The sun was shining and the water was blue and calm.

"What a perfect day for a party!" Frankie proclaimed.

Marcia and Lou quickly approached them, and Marcia gave Frankie a kiss on the cheek.

"My goodness, Frankie, you look wonderful! You seem twenty years younger! I have to have the name of your doctor."

Lou quickly stuck out his hand. "Hi, there! So glad you could join us." He turned towards Arnold.

"This is Arnold, my date for today," Frankie said, as the two men shook hands.

Marcia's eyes narrowed momentarily, as she looked at Arnold. A flash of recognition crossed her face and her eyes became as big as saucers. She quickly took in a deep breath.

"Pleasure to meet you both," Arnold said. He bent over to kiss Marcia's hand and gave her a quick wink and a smile.

"You, too," she answered with relief. "You two just make yourselves right at home. We're expecting our son any minute. "He'll be so surprised!"

Marcia clutched her husband's arm and gave him a beaming smile. "Oh, there are the Boyd's! I *have* to ask them about their gardener. Excuse us," she said to Frankie and Arnold.

Frankie began to giggle. "She went so white when she saw you, I thought she was going to faint."

Arnold laughed. He was used to the nervous stares and conspiratorial eyes he received when couples came into the store. It was as if the women were sending silent messages to him through telepathy. *"Don't let my husband know about the store room. Act like we've never spoken. Don't mention the new line of Gucci sunglasses."*

Of course, he would never do anything to jeopardize the wonderful enterprise that was thriving in the storeroom.

"Where exactly is their son coming from?" Arnold asked.

"That's the terrible part, Arnold. I've been such a recluse, I didn't even know they *had* a son. Of course, after the nice invitation, I was too embarrassed to ask. I'm guessing he's in the military. Maybe he's been in Iraq or Afghanistan. Why else would you have a coming home party? If he was coming home from college, you would have a graduation party, right?"

She held out a pretty wrapped package. "That's why I got him this commemorative coin for those who've helped to protect our country. It's really the first time I've purchased something for someone in the military. If I had known what branch of the military he's in, I could have been more specific. Do you think it'll be okay?"

"It sounds perfect, Frankie!"

"I hope so. Oh well, it's done now. No need to think further about it. Look, there are other gifts on that table over there. Shall we?"

***

Johnny rubbed his eyes his eyes and looked over at Trenton. He cleared his throat and sat up as straight as he could, given the brace on his back. According to the doctor, he still had to wear it for another few weeks.

"Hope Mom and Pops are ready for us. I haven't eaten in six hours."

"Knowing my mom," Johnny replied, "she'll have a full seven course meal ready for us."

"I could go for that."

When they pulled into the driveway, Trenton helped Johnny out of the car before heading to the trunk to grab their bags. As they walked slowly up the steps, Johnny wondered why his mother wasn't on the front porch looking anxious and relieved to have him back home. Quite unexpectedly, they walked into a deserted foyer.

"So much for a seven course meal," Trenton teased, as they both looked around for signs of Johnny's parents. The house was empty. "Are you sure they knew we were coming today?"

"I called them two days ago. They must be out by the pool."

The two of them stepped tentatively into the backyard . . . to be met by a loud chorus of "SURPRISE!"

Marcia and Lou descended on Johnny with open arms.

"There's my boy!" Lou exclaimed, hugging his son awkwardly, trying to avoid putting any pressure on his back brace.

Johnny immediately put his hands to the stubble on his own face. He hadn't shaved before they left the hospital. *How embarrassing,* he thought. He gave his mother a stern look. "Mom, I wasn't expecting a party."

"Oh honey, I know, but we're just so glad that our baby safely back at home. It is such a wonderful reason to celebrate!"

Johnny gathered himself and looked around the backyard. There must have been *two hundred* people scattered around. He shot them all a charming, yet humble smile and mouthed the words, "Thank you."

"Oh Johnny, why don't you introduce Trenton to everyone! You need to thank everyone for coming, too. Be a good host!" Marcia said. "Your father and I have to go talk to Father Tony."

She whisked Lou away and left Trenton and Johnny standing on the back porch. There was a jazz band playing music under the pergola, and the scent of boiled shrimp wafted towards them.

"Damn, man, my biggest home coming party was when I returned from college with a degree in my hand. All I got a pot of jambalaya and a list of chores that needed to be completed before I went to sleep!"

Johnny laughed. "Well, I guess it's time to mingle."

They made their way down the steps and onto the pool deck. Trenton protectively moved behind Johnny, in case he suddenly plummeted to the ground.

Frankie, who was standing next to Arnold at the opposite end of the pool, reached over and pinched his arm. "Oh shit! Where's his uniform?"

"I don't know. Maybe he's not in the military after all," Arnold replied.

Frankie eyed the present table, and immediately began working an angle for grabbing the present and stuffing it into her purse, before anyone could see it. Suddenly she gasped. The catering crew had just arrived and started clearing the table. They quickly whisked the presents away, and another set of waiters began setting up chafing dishes filled with steaming hot, aromatic food.

Arnold watched Frankie, a little worried that she might begin a crying spell like the one he had encountered in the store room. Frankie just started laughing, though. She started laughing so hard that her eyes were watering. The laughter was infectious, too. Before long, Arnold began grinning, and then laughing. In seconds, not only were both she and Arnold cracking up so much that people were starting to stare, the nice elderly couple next to them began snickering, as well. Soon after, their little snickers turned into chuckles. Then, those chuckles turned into full-out knee-slapping laughs. They didn't even know what they were laughing about! But as their bellies started to shake, they didn't care. Before long, everyone standing in that yard was laughing so hard, they could hardly catch their breath.

Trenton watched the scene with interest. "What did your parents put in the punch?"

As he waited for an answer, they approached Frankie and Arnold. Johnny didn't know either of them, and figured they worked with his father or maybe were members of the club. He hesitated in greeting them, because he didn't want to embarrass them. They both had tears rolling down their cheeks and didn't seem to be able to contain themselves. As he walked to them, they tried to straighten up and look serious. However, as Frankie and Arnold glanced at each other, the giggles started all over again.

Frankie was embarrassed at her display, but boy, did it feel good to her to just let go and laugh. She grabbed Johnny and Trenton in a big bear hug. Unlike Johnny's father, she wasn't awkward and gentle. She oozed affection and looked them both in the eyes, before saying, "Glad to meet you both. I'm Frankie Walters. I live next door. This is my friend, Arnold."

Arnold reached out to shake their hands. Johnny seemed like a nice guy, and would probably get a kick out of the medal Frankie was giving him. Arnold turned to Trenton, who cleared his throat and swallowed hard. His adam's apple bobbed, as he looked into Arnold's eyes. "Trenton Bertrand. Nice to meet you, Arnold."

Arnold nodded and was suddenly very conscious of his wet cheeks.

"Nice to meet you, too."

Frankie grabbed Johnny's arm and walked him over to a bench on the edge of the pool deck.

"Come on over here and sit down, Johnny. With that brace on your back, I'm guessing you feel better sitting down, rather than standing up."

"Thank you, Mrs. Walters."

"No, it's Frankie to you, unless you want me to start calling you Sergeant."

With that, the laughter started all over again. Frankie *did* manage to let Johnny and Trenton in on their faux pas. They enjoyed a wonderful evening together, filled with dancing and fun and newfound friendship. Late that night, as she laid her head down on the pillow in her own bedroom of her own house, Frankie said a silent prayer to Grams, thanking her for pushing her in the direction she obviously needed to go.

19 THANK YOU, DEAR GOD

Dear Lord,

I just wanted to come to you today to give you thanks for all you've given me. For my church home and family, includin' Reverend Sanders, Patsy, Mrs. Whipple, all the sweet little children, and even for Mandy and the quilting ladies. They all have their faults, just like I do. Just please help me to remember they are your children, too.

Thank you, too, dear God, for bringin' Wayne into my life. I never knew what I was missin' 'til now. I see why you put Eve in the garden with Adam. I see how someone else can make you feel whole, when you didn't even know you was missin' something.

Thank you for all the prayers you answer. Those I ask for me and those I ask for other people.

Please help those who ain't as lucky as me during this season. Be with those little children who are gonna' be gettin' one of our church stockings. I hope their little faces just light up when they get 'em. Help Drunk Joe and creepy Earl, too.

In your precious son's name, I pray, Amen.

20 THERE'S NO PLACE LIKE HOME —
GET ME THE HELL OUT OF HERE

Cindy and Luke celebrated after the parade. The fact is, they celebrated in the back seat of Cindy's car, in the field behind Luke's house, and in the town hall's bathroom. They danced the night away at the Biblesta Dance for Jesus. Cindy was on cloud nine. She had won first place and found Jesus, all in the span of one weekend. She had her prize money and could now make her pilgrimage to Florida, just like she'd planned for years. However, now Luke was in the picture. She wondered if he had ever thought about going to Florida . . . or even just getting out of Humboldt.

Cindy laughed, as she realized she was getting ahead of herself. It had only been three days. Maybe she would soon find out he wasn't perfect in every way. He *had* to have a flaw of some sort. She spent an hour looking for it that night, but saw nothing but perfection. He dropped her off at 2:00 a.m., and kissed her goodnight.

"Thank you for an amazing night, Cindy. Care to pick up again tomorrow? I'd love to take you out for a romantic dinner, just the two of us. Without crowds of people cheering for a parade and beer pong games in the other room."

"That sounds wonderful."

"I'll pick you up at 7:00 tomorrow, then." He walked her up to the door. The porch light was on and the curtains were open. They could see Uncle Ricky sitting in his recliner. Luke pecked her quickly on the cheek, winked and nodded at Uncle Ricky, and then waved goodbye.

Gorgeous . . . and a gentleman, too, she thought.

Cindy climbed into bed that night with a sense of calm, combined with nervous excitement. It was a feeling she had not felt before. A week earlier, all that had mattered was getting to Florida. Now, all she could think about was seeing Luke the next night. *Funny, the turns life takes*, she thought, as she drifted off into sleep.

Funny, however, turned to dread, as Uncle Ricky shook her from sleep two hours later.

"Wake up, baby!" he said.

"What is it, Uncle Ricky?" She got her answer, though, before he could say a word. The town's sirens were blaring. Cindy jumped from the bed and grabbed her robe. Aunt Nancy was opening all the windows. Uncle Ricky grabbed a flashlight and took Cindy by the hand.

"Come on, baby. Let's get down to the cellar."

When they ran across the yard, Cindy could see a green tint in the sky and felt the eerie, telltale wind picking up around her. Once safely inside the cellar, she felt herself release the breath she had been holding the whole way across the yard. Uncle Ricky turned on the radio and waited for news about the approaching storm. Aunt Nancy draped a blanket over Cindy's shoulders and put her hand on her knee. Cindy felt dog tired, given all the excitement leading up to the parade and the late night she'd spent with Luke. Laying her head on Aunt Nancy's lap, she drifted back to sleep, with Nancy gently rubbing her temples.

Ricky shook his head. "I'll be damned if this isn't the first time that girl's slept through a twister."

"Do you think she's okay?" Nancy asked.

"I think she's *better* than okay. I think she may just be in love. She was walking on air when she came in from her date with Luke. She looked like she had stars in her eyes."

Nancy smiled. "She deserves a nice young man to take her mind off of things."

After an hour, the National Weather Service discontinued the tornado warning for their area. Nancy gently woke Cindy and they headed back to the house. There wasn't much damage to their yard—just a few small limbs down and a flower pot on the front porch that had fallen over.

"How about I get a little ham and eggs going?" Nancy asked. "Cindy, you make the coffee. Let's start this morning over again, why don't we?"

"Sounds good," Cindy said. She filled the coffee filter and pushed the start button on the coffee maker.

As it was brewing, she turned on the small TV set on the kitchen counter. The local news crew appeared on the screen, reporting from around town with an update on damage done by the tornado.

"At approximately 4:14 a.m., the tornado touched down. Unfortunately, there was one fatality in the Humboldt area."

The camera panned a small white house with a tree laying on top of a collapsed roof.

"Oh my God, Luke!" she screamed. Uncle Ricky came running into the kitchen and stared at Cindy and then at the TV. "That's Luke's house!" Tears were pouring from her eyes. "I have to get over there!"

"Honey, I don't think that's such a good idea," he said, trying to calm her down. "Let's call Dan at the police station and see if we can get any information."

"No! I have to go . . . *now!*"

She grabbed her car keys.

"I'll take you," Uncle Ricky protested. "Give me the keys."

Running out the door and jumping into her car, they sped down County Road 315. Minutes later, as they pulled into Luke's driveway, they saw exactly what the TV had shown them — there were police cars and ambulances scattered around the yard. A local utilities truck was a short distance back, waiting its turn to get close enough to fix the fallen power line. Cindy ran into the yard and, upon seeing Luke's roommate, fell to her knees. She was glad *he* was okay, but that left only Luke! A police officer ran up to assist Uncle Ricky, as they pulled Cindy to her feet. Her whole body was shaking..

Without warning, a shot of adrenaline coursed through her blood and she broke free of their grasp, sprinting up the steps, through the front door and straight to the back of the house. The tree had fallen right where Luke's bedroom was. She rounded the corner and saw his dead body, his tanned arms stretched out wide. His long brown hair was disheveled and wet. The tree had pinned him onto his bed as he slept. The massive trunk lay directly upon his torso. However, Cindy could see his face and it looked so peaceful. She knelt down and prayed aloud to Jesus, or maybe it was to Luke. She wasn't sure. "*Why?*" she asked. "*Why*, Jesus?"

***

Now, two months later, as Cindy walked numbly into the house, Uncle Ricky followed behind with his lips tight. He wondered just how he was going to break the news to Nancy.

Cindy had taken her lunch break at the store. It was her first day back at work since Luke's death. She had taken a month off, and during that time, it was everything Nancy could do to even get her out of bed to eat. When she did eat, she couldn't keep anything down. Pastor Terry was Aunt Nancy's last resort.

One Sunday, she invited him to lunch after church. Once lunch was over, he knocked on Cindy's bedroom door and brought in a piece of Aunt Nancy's prize-winning pineapple upside down cake. Cindy groggily peered at him.

"Hi, Cindy. Brought you a piece of cake. It's like sunshine on a plate! Looks like you could use a little sunshine." He handed the cake to her and opened the blinds. Sitting on the end of her bed, he studied her thoughtfully.

"Luke was a good man, Cindy. Always willing to help around the church yard or cook pancakes at the men's breakfast. We miss him at the church, and I know you miss him, too."

He wanted the words to seep into her heart. Lesson number one for healing a hurt soul in your flock: acknowledge the sadness. Number two, remind them of God's unconditional love.

"God loves Luke, Cindy, just as He loves you. He had a bigger plan for Luke than what he could do here on earth. He called him to Heaven, because he needed him there."

"But we need him here in Humboldt. *I* need him," Cindy responded with tears in her eyes. "He was our Jesus. Who's going to be Jesus, now?"

Lesson number three appeared in Pastor Terry's mind: listen to their anger and hear their hurt. Acknowledge that those feelings are okay. "Just let it out, Cindy. Let it out."

Cindy cried and cried. She must have cried for twenty minutes, but Pastor Terry just patiently waited, until there seemed to be no tears left. Number four, give them hope.

"You and Luke are only separated here in your earthly life. When you are called to Heaven, I'm sure Luke will be there waiting for you."

The image clouding Cindy's mind, in that moment, was one of Luke standing bare-chested before her, with a light breeze blowing his hair away from his face. Added to that, she envisioned golden light radiating from his toned abs.

This has to be sacrilegious, she thought. However, as she sat on her bed with her eyes closed, she refused to let it fade. Cindy saw him smile and hold out his hand to her. She couldn't help but smile back, feeling more at peace than she had in a month.

Pastor Terry reached out and gently held her hands. As he did, the scene in her head fell away with her smile.

"Let's pray," Pastor Terry said. As he prayed for God to comfort Cindy, Cindy prayed she would never forget the vision she had just seen. She also prayed she would be in Florida by November.

***

During her first day back at work, as she hovered over the toilet seat in the drug store bathroom, Cindy put out another prayer. "Dear God, please help me."

As if in answer to her prayer, a second pink line appeared on the pregnancy test stick, looking so pretty and proud. She dropped her head. Although she was embarrassed and ashamed for having had sex with Luke -even before their first date, at that- there was a happiness tugging at her heart. She hadn't lost Luke completely. He left behind a part of himself inside of her.

Surely it was a gift from Luke *and* from God. She thought back to the stories Uncle Ricky had told her about her mother. He had described to her how excited she had been when she'd found out about Cindy. Smiling at the irony, Cindy decided then and there she wouldn't be ashamed or sorry for this gift.

She marched straight into Uncle Ricky's office and told him the news. *No need putting off the inevitable,* she thought. He was shocked, but he also knew how this worked, having already been through it once. Cindy had taught him what a blessing a surprise like this could be. He agreed with her, there was nothing to be sorry about. Giving Cindy a heartfelt hug, he promised that he and Nancy would be there for her and the baby.

"That's just the thing, Uncle Ricky. I know you and Aunt Nancy will always be there for me. I just can't stay here in Humboldt. I won't let this baby grow up without a mother. I won't let another tornado pull someone away from me. Me and this baby are going to get out of here and start a new life in Florida."

Ricky pulled his glasses from his face and looked down at his lap. *It won't do for her to see me crying*, he thought. Biting his lower lip, he took a deep breath through his nose. When he was composed, he looked at Cindy.

"We knew this day would come, baby. Can't say I'm happy about it though. But what kind of uncle would I be if I stood in the way of you and your dreams?"

"What kind of uncle? You're not my *uncle*. You're my *father*."

***

Arnold felt pity when Cynthia from Humboldt, Kansas walked up to the customer service desk and asked for a job application. She looked tired and distraught, even though she was a pretty girl. Her big brown eyes seemed far away. As he handed her an application, he said, "I actually just lost one of my cashiers. Kate moved to Key West with her boyfriend to start a charter fishing company. You're in luck."

"I'd call me just about anything but lucky."

165

Arnold smiled at her. "You ever worked in a store before?"

"I worked in my Uncle Ricky's drug store since I could walk."

"Well then, it sounds like you're certainly qualified for the position. Why don't you fill out the application and get it back to me. Then we can talk further. I could really use an extra body in here as quickly as possible."

"Well, I can start ringing items now. I've got nowhere else to go."

"Here, take a seat and grab one of those pens."

After Cindy finished the application, Arnold did a quick background check and was satisfied she would be a nice addition to his staff. She seemed genuine and loyal, two qualities Arnold looked for in an employee. Another thought crossed his mind: the party at Frankie's house was only a few days away. He would need staff to help pull sizes and ring up the ladies. *This girl*, he thought, *is beautiful and well-spoken. She'll also look great modeling some of the clothes.*

"Well, Cindy, welcome to Shop and Save. I'd be happy to go ahead and begin your paperwork. Then, Ellen can show you around and give you the grand tour. Come on back with me to my office, just this way. You look like you'll fit into Kate's uniform. Size 4, if my guess is correct?"

Cindy seemed slightly taken aback at his accuracy. She nodded and suddenly began to cry. Her doe-like eyes brimmed over with tears. She sniffed and tried to hide her face. *This is definitely not the way to impress your boss on your first day of work,* she thought. "Sorry," she said quietly.

Arnold normally didn't allow his employees in on the Shop & Save business, until he was sure he could trust them; but there was something about Cindy telling him it would be okay. He also realized he couldn't have her sobbing in the middle of the soda aisle. He made a quick decision to grab a bottle of wine, as they passed the wine display. He knew now, from experience, that crying women needed wine. Cindy was crying so hard, she didn't even notice.

Arnold unlocked the door and held out his arm. "Cindy, sit here and let me get you a tissue. I bet the things in here will raise your spirits." He pulled a tissue from a box on a table and passed it to her. She blew her nose and looked around.

"What *is* this place?"

"Well, it's a little Shop and Save secret that you are *now* in on. I'll tell you all about it. You see, we have a little underground shopping experience going here at Shop & Save. Our customers are privy to the latest fashions. Take this, for example. The lead singer from Fight or Flight was just interviewed wearing this necklace. Try finding it anywhere else in Jacksonville."

He held up a black leather band with a crucifix hanging from it. Cindy took one look at the cross and the heavenly figure hanging from it and fell apart. The tears earlier were nothing compared to the full-body shaking that immediately commenced. Her shoulders heaved and the sobs became louder and louder. Arnold worriedly looked around and contemplated what to do. *The wine!* he thought. He opened the bottle and offered it to Cindy.

She managed to utter the words, "I can't," through her tears.

"*Sure* you can. It's okay, Cindy. Maybe it'll calm you down."

"No, I mean, I can't!" The tears came harder. "I can't because it's not healthy . . . for the baby."

At that, Arnold sat down and threw up his hands. A hormonal pregnant woman who couldn't be comforted with wine was new territory. He took a giant swallow himself and decided to patiently wait her out. After about ten more minutes, she seemed to have nothing left. She looked at Arnold with an embarrassed look.

"Mr. Arnold, I'm so sorry. I am usually very professional. My Uncle Ricky always taught me that customer service makes a store. That means always keeping your calm. I didn't mean to lose it like that. You just caught me on a bad day. I really *do* want to work for you. If you'll give me a chance, I promise there will be no tears spilt on the scanner."

"I believe you, Cindy," Arnold said, pausing to gather himself after her obviously sincere apology. "Why don't you tell me what's happened to you to make you so sad. Maybe there's something I can do to help you out."

After a box of Kleenex for Cindy and a bottle of wine for Arnold, Cindy had spilled her life story. Arnold was amazed at how strong she seemed, for all that had happened. And now, she was going to have a baby, *and* raise him or her in a strange place.

Cindy felt like she had found an ally in Arnold. The fact that her new boss had finished a bottle of wine with her in a back store room would usually have put her on alert, but she felt safe with him—like he was a friend, instead of a strange man. After an hour and a half, Cindy's paperwork was completed, her name tag was made, and she had her uniform in her arms.

"See you in the morning, Cindy."

"Thank you again, Arnold. For the job and for the ear."

As Cindy left the office, Arnold scanned the paperwork. She had listed the Gator Lodge as a temporary place of residence. That was not in the best section of town. He shook his head. It just wasn't safe for a girl her age to be around the kind of people who hung out at the Gator Lodge. As he was wondering about a possible solution, the phone rang. He could see from the caller I.D. that it was Frankie. After his greeting, she began to spew forth details about the upcoming party. His mind tried to keep up, but his thoughts were still glued to poor Cindy's predicament.

"I've got enough room to set up twenty dressing rooms. Do you think we need more?" Frankie asked.

Something clicked, and suddenly Arnold latched onto what he thought might be a perfect solution.

"Frankie, I just hired a new cashier to replace Kate. She's a real sweet girl from Kansas, and she's pregnant. She seems like she could use a friend or two. The father of her baby was killed in a tornado, and she packed up and moved here to get away."

"That's terrible. Of *course* she'll need friends. Having a baby on your own isn't easy. Does she need maternity clothes? What about pre-natal vitamins? Does she even have a doctor here in town?"

"Well, I don't think so. She just got into town a few days ago. I think more than anything, she could use a place to stay for a while. She's at the Gator Lodge, now."

"No! That place won't do. She'll stay with me."

"Are you sure, Frankie?"

"Without a shadow of a doubt! She can stay in the pool house, so she'll have some privacy. We can't let her spend one more night there. I'll be at the store in ten minutes, and we'll get her packed and over here tonight."

With that, Frankie hung up the phone and bolted to the kitchen table to retrieve her purse and car keys. Arnold had locked the store for the night, and in minutes was waiting at her front door.

Once Frankie got into the car, Arnold glanced at her with an unsure look.

"Are you sure this is okay, Frankie? I didn't mean to put you on the spot. She seems like a sweet girl, but what if there's an ax murderer hiding underneath that slow Kansas accent?"

"Oh really, Arnold! I'm sure that if you approved of her enough to hire her, she'll be just *fine*. I've got more room in that house than I know what to do with! I might as well share a little piece of it, if I can. Now, tell me, what's her story?"

On the way to the Gator Lodge, Arnold relayed as many of the details to Frankie as he could. By the time they pulled into the parking lot, Frankie had a tear running down her cheek and a look of resolve on her face. She marched up to the bulletproof glass window and asked that the clerk ring Cindy's room. She motioned for Arnold to come to the phone. After a few minutes, the door to room 28 swung open. Cindy was clutching a bathrobe around her waist. Arnold made the introductions, and it took Frankie exactly 18 minutes to convince Cindy this wasn't a place in which she should stay. It took Frankie another 10 minutes to convince her to accept her invitation. Uncle Ricky and Aunt Nancy would be appalled if they knew Cindy had even gotten into the car with someone she didn't know, much less spent the night in their house. But Cindy felt safe with Arnold, just as she had in the store, and Frankie was as nice as anyone she knew back home.

"I don't take charity, Frankie. So, you'll have to let me pay you."

"Okay," Frankie replied. "How much are you paying to stay here a night?"

"Thirty dollars," she answered.

"My place is thirty dollars a week. Take it or leave it."

There was something about Frankie's demeanor that told Cindy she would be fighting a losing battle if she tried to argue. But she dug in her heels.

"Fine, but I'll be doing some cooking and cleaning to help you out."

"It's settled, then. Arnold, would you mind grabbing her suitcase there?"

21 THE FIVE PLAGUES OF CHRISTMAS

*I always get real excited around Christmas. Knowin'
that God's son came to earth on that day just gives me
goosebumps. Wayne just hung the garland in the church,
and the quilting ladies just put all the ornaments on the tree.*

*I started my Christmas shopping early this year.
Usually, I only have a few gifts to buy-one for Reverend
Sanders, one for Elaine, the mail lady, and one for Dee over
at the diner. I also always send all of my clients a cross-stitch
book mark. Mrs. Harry, who lives a few trailers down, makes
them for me each year. In exchange, I give her free rent for
the month of December. I change up the design every year, in
case I'm still prayin' for somebody who I was prayin' for the
previous year. Then, there's always the bottle of liquor I take
over to Drunk Joe, although he moved from the post office to
the dry cleaners. The little Korean lady who works there
doesn't speak English, so I don't think she can do anything*

about him. Ain't nobody understands her if she does try to complain.

I started taking Drunk Joe liquor about four years ago. It was real cold on Christmas Eve, and I saw him sittin' there outside . . . and felt real sorry for him. I hadn't ever tried to talk to him again, since I was little. But something just told me that a drink would warm him up. So I walked into the liquor store, which I ain't ever done before, and bought him Old Granddad, on account of he looks like somebody's old ornery granddad. He looked at me real strange, when I held the bottle out to him.

"Ain't you that retarded girl?" he asked me.

I told him I was just passin' by and thought he might like some whisky. He took it real quick and stuck it under the coat that was coverin' his legs.

"Go on, now, get!" he said.

I moved on and said a special prayer for him on that Christmas Eve. I've been visitin' him every Christmas Eve since.

This year, I got to add Wayne to my Christmas list. I've never had to buy a Christmas gift for a boyfriend. I spent a lot of weeks wonderin' what to get for him. What do you get somebody who has been as good to me as Wayne has? After three months of just kissin', I decided to give him "the gift" I know he wants more than anything: me. I planned a night of pure romance with candles, wine coolers and new lace panties. Well, I'll tell you, what I gave him wasn't at all what I had planned.

I reckon that God was tryin' to tell me that havin' sex before marriage wasn't such a good idea. He sure made his message loud and clear.

It started two days before Christmas Eve. I was dreaming I was walking through Wal-Mart. This little old lady walked by and she had something stuck to the bottom of her shoe. I could hear her coming down the aisle. I was picking out a new lip gloss, and she came scratching along. She stopped where I was and asked if I could pray for her. She said she couldn't seem to walk quietly anymore. She said her feet made so much noise, now that she was older. That's when I looked down, and she had a big ol' stick reachin' out from under her shoe. I told her she didn't need a prayer; she just needed somebody to pull the stick off of her shoe. I bent down and lifted her foot and pulled the stick away. She smiled and thanked me. But then, when she walked away, the sound was still there. Not only was it still there, it got louder! I reckon' that's what pulled me out of my deep sleep. As I opened my eyes, it seemed weird I could still hear the old woman scraping along.

As I pulled myself awake, I realized there really was a scratching noise, and it was coming from under my bed. I leaned my ear over the edge of the bed and lay real still. There it was again. That's when I turned on my lamp and held it down so the light shone under the bed. As I did, I saw a rat. I nearly jumped off the bed, but caught myself. Instead, I started jumping on the bed, hopin' to scare him out of there. I don't know if that little thing was scared himself or if he was just dumb, but he didn't move. If he wadn't movin', I wadn't movin', either. So, there we both sat. I didn't sleep another wink that night. I called Wayne as early as I thought I could, which was around 5:30. He came over and shooed that rat right out from under the bed. He ran across the floor and Wayne chased him, until he disappeared behind the refrigerator. That didn't sit too well with me. I knew he was still in my trailer.

Wayne could see my distress, so he went out as soon as the hardware store opened and got some rat poison. He explained to me the rats will eat the poison and then get real thirsty. When they drink the water, that's when they die. As much as I hate to kill one of God's creatures, I hate to have them runnin' around in my house even more. So with the poison set out, and no sign of the rat slippin' into my bathroom, I took my shower and got dressed. I was going to help the children's choir try on their costumes for the Christmas pageant. We have lots of shepherd costumes, angel wings, and wise men crowns we've used over the years – quite a selection, I must say. Each year, a few days before Christmas, the kids come to the church to pick out their costumes and have hot chocolate, followed by the dress rehearsal. I helped little one after little one try on robes and headdresses, until they each found somethin' they liked that fit.

By the time I was finished, I was more tired than I figured I should be. I went home and plopped onto the sofa. Wayne had come over to watch a football game. I fell right asleep. After the game was over, Wayne came over to give me a goodbye kiss. He shook me awake and told me I was burnin' up with fever. He got me some aspirin and Gatorade and helped me into bed.

"You want me to stay here with you, darlin'?" he asked.

I felt bad asking him to sleep on the sofa, but I was feelin' so sick that I was scared to be alone. Like always, Wayne helped me out. When the mornin' came, and I was still feelin' feverish, he loaded me up in his pick-up and took me to the emergency clinic. By this time, my head and my throat was achin' something awful. After swabbin' my throat, they told me I had strep throat. They gave me a prescription for some medicine and told me to get lots of rest. That is just what I was aimin' to do, until we walked into my trailer. On the floor, scattered around my livin' room, were six baby rats! Two was right out dead, but the other four were kinda' breathin' heavy and tryin' to move, but gettin' nowhere fast. I swear I nearly died.

Wayne shoved them out of the way with his foot and helped me to bed. He told me he would take care of the rats. I didn't have the strength to argue, so I let him. I slept all that day and then all night, too. I woke up around 7:30 the next morning. I could tell my fever was gone, because I wasn't freezin' no more. I carefully made my way out of the bedroom, watching out for rats. I didn't see any. But, I did see Wayne sound asleep on my sofa. I tiptoed over and shook him. As he woke up, he looked at me real funny. I went to give him a hug, and he backed up real quick.

"What's wrong?" I asked.

"Babe, you might want to go look into the mirror."

I ran to the bathroom, and there were big ol' gross sores all over my face. I reached up to touch one and noticed they were on my arms, as well. Wayne walked up behind me with his truck keys and my coat.

"Let's go back to the doctor," he said.

I wasn't about to argue. I looked disgusting. As we rode down the road, I let my hair fall in front of my face, so he couldn't see the scabs poppin' up all around my mouth and nose.

The doctor took one look at me and told me I had impetigo, somethin' that goes with strep sometimes. They gave me some cream to put on the sores and sent me home again.

It was one day before Christmas Eve, and I was in bad shape. My new panties were still hidden in a bag in the back of my closet, along with the wine coolers, which should have been chillin' in the refrigerator. Lookin' at myself in the side mirror of his truck, I was thinkin' that sex is probably the last thing he would think about when he looked at those scabs. When we got back home, he helped me inside and got me all tucked into bed. He turned on the TV for me and got me a glass of water.

I knew then why they say "in sickness and in health" in the wedding vows. Life just wouldn't be so good without somebody to help you through things like this. He reached over and squeezed my hand.

"You need anything else?" he asked. "I've got a few jobs I need to finish before tomorrow night. Mrs. Elise is gonna' be pretty mad, if I don't get her guest bathroom toilet unclogged before her daughter gets home for Christmas."

I told him I was just fine and sent him on his way. I remember sleepin' throughout the day again. I would wake up here and there, take a sip of my drink, watch a few minutes of TV, and then drift back off to sleep. That night, Wayne came over to check on me. It was Christmas Eve, and the wine coolers were still hot. He brought a couple of frozen pizzas with him. It wadn't the fanciest Christmas Eve dinner, but it sure tasted good, since I had hardly eaten in two days. He pulled out a little package after dinner. It was wrapped in green foil paper with a little red bow on the top. I ain't never felt so bad in my life! I looked at him and just burst out cryin'.

"That isn't quite the reaction I expected," he said.

"It's not your gift, Wayne. It's just that I cain't give you your gift tonight. I'm so sorry," I sobbed.

He told me to go ahead and open his gift. I did and it made me cry even harder. It was a beautiful little blown glass angel. He said he saw it and right off knew it was meant for me. He hugged me and then pushed me back from him a bit. With the crusty sores on my face, I can't say I blame him.

Once I got myself together enough to talk, he looked at me with those big brown eyes of his. "Hey Babe, just wonderin', what was it that you were going to give to me?"

I looked at him right in the eyes and smiled.

"I was going to give you me, Wayne. All of me. But, then I got sick and now look at me. I know that crawlin' in bed with me lookin' like this is the last thing a man would want."

"Babe, you look good to me anytime. But, you need to rest and get better. We'll have time. Maybe we can start the new year off with a bang!" He winked at me, then he stood up and paced back and forth in front of the TV. He looked like he was ponderin' something real hard. He stopped and looked at me.

"I do have something that I want for Christmas, babe, other than you. I've been trying to figure out another way, but I just can't find one."

"What is it?"

"There's this family back where I come from, the Millers. They have always been real good to me. They took me in when my momma went on one of her drinking binges. Their son, who died in Afghanistan, while serving our country, gave me his hand-me-downs when we were little and I didn't have shoes to wear. Over the years, they gave and gave without asking for anything in return. I hadn't been in touch with them for a while, but I called this morning to wish them a merry Christmas. I found out, by talking to Mrs. Miller, that their house burned down two weeks ago. They didn't have insurance, and they lost everything. They're staying in a hotel, now, and it's just breaking my heart. They need some money to start over. I would give em' everything I have, but I ain't got much."

I told Wayne how sorry I was for his friends. I told him I would gladly help anyone who helped shape him into the wonderful man he is today. He told me they could move into a government subsidized house with a $10,000 down payment.

"Wouldn't it be something special to show up at their door with the check wrapped in a Christmas bow?" he said.

Although, the selfish me wanted him to spend Christmas with me, I knew in my heart that his idea was a good one. Had I not been so sickly, I would have gone with him. I'd have loved to see the look on their faces. But as it was, I was stuck at home. I told Wayne he should go first thing in the morning. He'd be there by noon on Christmas day, if he left early. We turned on It's a Wonderful Life and had a cup of eggnog together. I felt warm and happy in my soul. Even though I knew my bank account would be real low, I knew that me and Wayne would be rewarded with riches in the afterlife.

Wayne left the trailer about 11:30 that night. He told me he would call me as soon as he delivered the check. I had transferred the money into his account, so he could write the check for the Millers. I got in bed and said a special prayer for all my clients, for the Millers, and a thank you for Wayne.

The next morning, I woke up, plugged up my little Christmas tree and ate a bowl of cereal. My face was looking better. My head was itching somethin' bad, though – so bad, I could barely stop clawing at it. As I finished my breakfast, Mrs. Sullivan knocked on my door. She had brought over some Christmas cookies.

"I ran into Wayne last night as he was leaving. He told me you were under the weather. I thought you might like some cookies to cheer you up," she said.

"Come on in," I told her. "I'll make us some hot chocolate." Mrs. Sullivan, like me, was usually all alone on Christmas. We always made a point of visiting for a bit on Christmas day. As she sat chatting, I just couldn't stop scratchin' my head.

"Honey, you got somethin' wrong with your head?"

"It's itchin' somethin' awful."

"Let me have a look," she said, as she stood up and came over to stand behind my chair. She began pushin' my hair from one side to the other.

"Grace, I'm sorry to tell you this, seein' as how you're still recoverin' from your sickness; but honey, you've got lice."

"Lice?"

"Yep, I used to see it all the time when I taught kindergarten. You got the lice and the knits, the eggs. You just need a lice kit from the drugstore. Just wash your bedding and use the kit. You'll be good as new."

The thought of those little critters crawling through my hair was about enough to put me over the edge. Rats, strep, impetigo and now lice! God sure was tryin' to get my attention. The drug store was closed for Christmas, so I had to wait it out. I busied myself for the rest of the day, cleanin' up and prayin' for my clients. Just because it was Christmas didn't mean that prayers weren't heard or answered. I also added the Millers to my daily prayer list. Around 4:00, I still hadn't heard from Wayne. I tried his cell phone, but didn't get an answer. I didn't think too much of it, though. He and the Millers probably had a lot to catch up on. But by 9:00 that night, I still hadn't heard from him. I fell asleep with the phone in my hand.

When I woke up the next morning and still didn't have a call or message from Wayne, I began to get worried. What if he had been in a car accident or something? I told myself God had surely delivered him safely to the Millers. He was just caught up in helpin' them. I decided to go about my daily business. I knew it would be real nice to get rid of my lice before Wayne returned. I didn't want to put that poor man through any more than I'd already put him through with my strep throat and all. So, I went to the drug store for *the lice kit. On the way home, I went to drop off Drunk Joe's whisky and apologize for not getting it to him on Christmas Eve. He reached his hand out, but then looked at the scabs on my face and shook his head. He pulled his hand back.*

"What's wrong with you now, girl? You got the pox or something?"

"Naw, just a little impetigo. That's all."

"You contagious?"

"Maybe a little."

"Well, you can just set it down over there," he said, pointing at the steps. "I'll get it later."

I set it down and wished him a merry Christmas.

My next stop was the post office. I hadn't picked up mail in a few days, so my P.O. Box was full. As I shuffled through the letters, I noticed one of my Christmas bookmarks had been returned. As I looked at the address, I saw it was from Ware State Prison. In red ink, it read: No longer incarcerated at Ware State Prison.

That made no sense. We had just emailed each other a few days earlier. He'd told me the prison was showing The Bells of Saint Mary's on Christmas Eve. He'd said they were going to have hotdogs and popcorn, like at a real movie. As I made my way back home, I figured the prison must have made some sort of mistake in their mail room.

So, when I got home, I called the prison and asked about Drew. The operator confirmed that Drew had been released three months earlier. I couldn't make sense of it. But, my head was still itching and I was gettin' a headache. I needed to get home and get myself back in order. I figured that Wayne would be home anytime, so I began pouring the bottle of lice killer on my head and took to combing out the knits. With any luck at all, and a few prayers, Wayne wouldn't have to know nothin' about the lice.

22 PREPARATIONS MAKE THE HEART GROW FONDER

It was hard for Cindy to believe she had been living with Frankie for three weeks already. Florida was an exotic place to live, compared to Kansas. Even though it was December, it was sixty-five degrees outside and sunny. And not only had there *not* been any tornadoes, there hadn't even been a rain shower.

As she walked downstairs for breakfast, Cindy put her hand on her stomach. She was just beginning to show. Frankie saw her rubbing her stomach and smiled. "Come on in and get some breakfast. I made waffles with strawberries. You need your folic acid, according to your pregnancy book."

"Thank you, Frankie. But *I'm* supposed to be the one helping *you* out. Remember our deal? Part of the rent payment?"

"Oh, hush. You being here is payment enough. I was by myself for so many years, I'm on cloud nine to have a sweet roommate like you."

They both heard a knock on the front door.

"Oh, that's probably Arnold," Frankie said. "He's stopping by to confirm all the trunk show details. I can't believe it's almost here!"

Arnold walked in and smiled at Frankie and Cindy. "You two look lovely this morning."

"Oh, Arnold, aren't you sweet," replied Frankie. "Sit down and let me get you a plate. We've got lots to talk through."

As Arnold and Cindy ate their breakfast, Frankie grabbed a cup of coffee and pulled out a notebook. She began spouting off a to-do list.

"Okay, first things first. Arnold, do you have a final guest count?"

"It looks like it will be around eighty-five or so."

"Wonderful!" Frankie said, clapping her hands together. "It's going to be fabulous. Now the caterer will be here tomorrow around 9:30 to start setting up the buffet. The mirrors are being delivered at the same time. I've hired a local design company to set up the dressing room curtains. The flowers will be delivered this afternoon."

"Frankie," Arnold interrupted, "you really don't need to go through so much trouble."

"Trouble? Honey, trouble was what I was going through before I met you two. This is nothing but fabulous!"

"Cindy, I hope you don't mind, but I've made an appointment for you and I to get our hair and nails done around 1:30. We should be back by 3:00 to finish setting up."

"Frankie, I couldn't. I'm fine. You go and I'll hold down the fort here."

"Nope. You're going and that's final." She looked at Arnold and smiled. "I've asked Johnny from next door to come over and supervise in my absence. I stopped over to visit yesterday, and I think his poor mother is smothering him to death. He and his friend Trenton will help out for as long as we need them."

At the mention of Trenton's name, Arnold's attention perked up a bit. Frankie gave him a wink. "Nice young men, they are," she said. She looked over at Cindy. "Johnny is quite a handsome young man. You two might just hit it off."

Cindy blushed. "Frankie, I'm definitely not what a man is looking for."

Frankie waved her hand in the air nonchalantly. "Oh, you're right, a beautiful, young, smart woman who is good down to the soul. I don't know why anyone would be interested in someone like that."

Cindy decided it would be best to let Frankie have her matchmaking fantasy. However, she was convinced a single pregnant woman was far from what a wealthy, handsome man would be looking for.

Arnold and Cindy left for work at the Shop and Save, while Frankie busied herself with the party preparations. When Cindy walked into the house that evening, she gasped. The house had been transformed into something truly stunning! There were vases of pink, orange and yellow tulips scattered throughout the foyer and living rooms. Elegant, pastel colored candles had been perfectly placed all around. Cindy had never been to a party of any kind *nearly* as elaborate as this. Frankie walked in and was glowing herself.

"What do you think?" she asked. "Do we need more candles?"

"Frankie, it's beautiful! Absolutely *beautiful*. How in the world did you do all this?"

"Parties are my thing, darling."

"You can say that again!"

Cindy had felt somewhat strange around Frankie, since she'd moved in with her. It was odd being thrown into a living situation with someone she didn't even know. Frankie had done nothing to contribute to the awkwardness, though. She had been gracious, kind and patient, even though Cindy was somewhat tight-lipped about her situation. However, as she looked around and saw the passion and joy Frankie had for life, she felt like she herself had something to live for. Frankie had been living alone, yet she was so happy. Cindy suddenly realized that life was going to be okay for her and the baby. She ran to Frankie and threw her arms around her neck.

"Thank you," she said, with tears of joy running down her face.

Frankie hugged her tight. "You're going to be just fine, baby. Now that we're friends, I'm going to see to that. Wipe those eyes, now. We can't be puffy tomorrow." She led her to the kitchen and began ladling soup into a bowl. "Eat now," she said. "That little one needs to eat."

23 PAIN, SORROW & LEGS SPREADIN'

It was three-thirty in the morning and Wayne still wasn't home, and he still wouldn't answer his phone. I had dozed off on the sofa, while I was prayin' for Johnny's lost girl. I thought I heard a car door outside the trailer, so I jumped up and ran to the door. It was somebody pullin' into Marla's driveway a few doors down. I called Wayne again and went straight to his voicemail. I decided that was it. I was going to get in my car and drive to the Miller's if I had to. Only problem was, I didn't know where they lived. Come to think of it, I didn't even know the name of the town where Wayne had grown up. I knew it was somewhere in Georgia, but that was all I knew. I turned my computer on and waited for it to boot up. I was usually pretty good at navigating my way around the internet. Hopefully, I could find some information about the fire.

After nearly an hour of scrollin' and Googlin', I was right back where I started. There wadn't mention of a fire anywhere. Then, finally, at about 4:15, my phone rang. I took a deep breath and said a thank you to God. I said hello, but the voice that came back to me wasn't Wayne's.

"Hello, Grace?"

"Yeah? Who is this?"

"This is Mandy."

I wondered what in the world Mandy would be callin' me for at this hour, and I asked her as much.

"I was wondering, um, if Wayne is there by any chance?"

"Wayne, what do you need Wayne for? Is your hot water heater broke again?"

"My hot water heater?"

"Yeah, didn't Wayne say it was your hot water heater he fixed a few weeks ago?"

"Oh, um, yes. It was my hot water heater. Yes, it's broken again. May I speak with Wayne?"

"He ain't here, Mandy. As a matter of fact, I cain't find him myself. He left first thing Christmas morning to go back to his hometown to take money to some friends of his who lost their home in a fire. I hadn't heard from him since then. I was just searching the internet tryin' to figure out what to do next."

There was a long pause on the phone.

"Mandy, you still there?"

"Yes, I am. Um, Grace, do you think I could come over?"

I nearly fell off my chair. Mandy comin' into Happy Meadows was like the Queen of England walkin' into the Piggly Wiggly grocery store. I still had scabs on my face, too. I sure didn't want her seeing me any worse off than I usually felt around her. So, I asked her why she wanted to come over.

"I just need to speak with you for a few minutes. I'll be over in ten."

I started to tell her that now just wasn't a good time, but the phone clicked and she was gone.

I quickly threw on some clean sweatpants and a sweater and lit the gardenia scented candle I'd bought for mine and Wayne's "first time." Unfortunately, the trailer still had the slight odor of dead rats. Then, I went into the bathroom and tried real hard to cover the bumps on my face with powder.

I wished I'd been able to drink coffee, then I would have put on a fresh pot, like they do on TV whenever a guest is comin' over. Instead, I opened the refrigerator to take stock of what I might offer a guest.

About that time, there was a knock on the door. I opened it and looked at Mandy. She looked worse than I did. She had dark circles under her eyes, and sores all over her face and neck. I was so stunned, I didn't even speak. After a few seconds of me standin' there like a statue, she said, "Hey, can I come in?"

I stood to the side and let her come in.

"Mandy, you have impetigo, too?"

"Yes, I look terrible. I've been embarrassed to step foot outside of my house."

"You didn't help at the nativity costume fittin', did you? I don't remember seeing you there."

"No, I didn't."

"Well, I just figured that's where I caught this mess, including the lice I just treated."

"Lice?" she asked. With that, she started scratchin' at her head at the thought of those little things. "You may have, but I caught it from somewhere else,"

"It must be like an epidemic spreadin' through our town," I figured out loud.

"Or, some epidemic whose been spreading legs through our town."

I must have looked pretty shocked. I wadn't quite sure what Mandy was talkin' about, and I didn't think a lady like her would say somethin' crude like that. Of course, after hearin' it, my curiosity was high.

"Come on in and sit down," I told her. "You want somethin' to drink? I've got Dr. Pepper and Gatorade."

"No, thank you. After what I tell you, you may not want to sit and enjoy a beverage with the likes of me."

So with that, I sat down in a chair across from her and waited.

"Grace, I know that you and Wayne have had something going on between the two of you for a while."

I nodded. I was always proud about havin' Wayne as my boyfriend.

"Grace, I've been seein' Wayne, too."

"Oh, you mean your counselin' appointments with Reverend Sanders? I know all about them. Wayne don't keep no secrets from me."

"Counseling appointments with Reverend Sanders? Dear God, is that what he told you? Honey, where we went, no God fearing man would go. Believe me, Reverend Sanders was nowhere near the two of us when we were together."

I stared at her tryin' to make sense of what she was saying. Mandy stared at me with wide eyes, waitin'.

"Grace, do I need to spell it out for you? Wayne has been with me for nearly two months. I know you thought you two had something, but he has been sleeping in my bed every night. Did you ever even wonder where his place was? Where he went when he left your house? I'll tell you. He came straight to mine."

I felt like my heart was bein' ripped from inside me. There had to be a mistake! What was she talking about? Wayne was sent to me by God! He was my soul mate! I was going to give myself to him… all of myself!

"You must be mistaken," I told her. "Wayne wouldn't no more do that to me than the man in the moon."

"Honey, you don't have to believe me, if you don't want to . . . but he's been playing you for the fool. Me, too, for that matter. He told me he felt sorry for you and that he was trying to help you get through some tough times. He promised me that ya'll weren't sleeping together or anything. Just a friend helping a friend."

"A friend? Mandy, he told me he loved me. I told him he was the one sent to me by God. You have got to be mistaken."

"Look, you said you gave him money to take to a friend, right? How much money did you give him?"

"That ain't really none of your business, Mandy," I shot back. I wadn't in the mood to hear anymore.

"Look, Grace, do you want to find Wayne or not? I think I've got a good idea of where he is."

With that, I burst out cryin'. Breakin' down in front of Mandy was about the last thing in the world I wanted to do. She stared at me and shook her head.

"You really love him, huh? I'll tell you what. Why don't you come over to my place, and I'll explain as much as I know," she offered.

At first, I felt like taking a swing at her, just to let her know how I felt. But then, I thought better about it, and decided to find out what else she might know that I didn't.

"Let me just grab my phone, in case he calls."

She looked at me with pity in her eyes. "Honey, he's not going to be calling you again."

Mandy drove us over to her house. I couldn't even speak. Between the tears streamin' down my face and the thoughts runnin' around in my head, I was a plain

190

ol' mess. Mandy didn't seem to mind, though. She just drive on and let me have some time.

We pulled into her driveway, and she told me to come on inside. She went right over to her fancy coffeemaker and started making up a fresh pot. "Seems like we could both use a cup of coffee," she said. I shook my head no. "Suit yourself."

After she poured herself a cup, she grabbed an envelope from the counter and sat down next to me. "He left this envelope in his drawer."

"His drawer?" I asked. "He had a drawer here?"

"Yeah, I told you he stayed here."

I felt like I was in a nightmare. How could I have not seen all this? She opened the envelope and shoved the contents toward me. "His drawer is empty, now," she spat. He cleaned it out while I was asleep. I guess he somehow missed this envelope, since he was packing in the dark-sneaking out like a crook in the middle of the night."

The first piece of paper was just a letter about some business in the Dominican Republic, but my breath caught as I saw the second piece of paper. It was a release paper from Ware State Prison dated September 1st. It just didn't make no sense. Why would Wayne have papers from Ware State Prison? I looked over at Mandy.

"I don't understand this?"

"Well, it looks like our lover boy was nothing but a criminal," Mandy answered.

I shook my head as I struggled to figure out what was happening. Even though I tried real hard to keep my prayers in the closet, I needed to tell Mandy about my prayer business. I told her about my client from Ware State Prison, and how I felt that God had sent Wayne to me as an answer to my prayers — as my soul mate, the one put on this earth just for me.

She grabbed the stack of papers. "The name on the release paper here is Drew. Ring a bell?" she asked.

As I shook my head up and down, her eyebrows furrowed. "Do you do pretty well with your prayer business? I mean, do you make good money?"

"Yeah, I guess so. Enough to keep the trailer park runnin' and to take care of myself."

"Did you share any of this with Drew? Maybe in one of your emails? Did you let him know about the trailer park? How about the prayer business? Did he know how much you charge for your prayers?"

My heart began to sink right into my chest. I thought of Drew as a friend. I had told him a lot about myself, now that I thought about it.

"Listen, Grace. You're a real nice girl. Nice girls make easy targets. I should know. I've hurt enough of them myself. He had your number, and he used it to make off with $10,000. The question is, are you going to keep on being the nice girl . . . or are you going to get a backbone and find him?"

As I sat there, two things came to my mind: one- turn the other cheek and two- vengeance is mine. I knew I should just go home. Pray for strength and continue on with my life. But at that moment, I was consumed with anger . . . and with sorrow. I asked Mandy to drive me home.

As I watched the trees go by, Mandy rattled on about things Wayne had said to her, the way he looked at her, like she was the only one in the world. All the things I wouldv'e swore he only did to me. By the time I got home, I felt forsaken by God. I also felt like a big old fool. How could I be so stupid to think that God would send someone just for me? God wadn't listenin' to me. I didn't have his ear. What a joke, that I charged money for prayers that weren't even bein' heard!

Well, I wadn't going to play the fool anymore. I was going to get my money from Wayne or Drew, or whoever he was. I packed my bags and scribbled down the return address on the letter from his cousin. That seemed like as good a place as any to start.

I drove all the way straight through to Florida. The anger inside of me was all I needed to keep me awake. Somethin' had shifted inside of me — whether what I was doin' was good or bad didn't matter anymore. I got to the Shop and Save at four-thirty in the afternoon, waltzed right up to the customer service department and asked to speak to the manager. The lady behind the desk told me that he wadn't going to be in today. She looked at me sorta' funny.

"You don't need guava jelly and persimmons do you?" she asked. "If so, I can give you the address where you can find him."

The grocery stores in Florida sure seemed a little crazy. But I didn't care what I had to say, as long as I could find Wayne's good-for-nothin' cousin.

"Actually, I do need them," I answered.

She smiled back at me real sweet. She wrote an address down on a piece of paper and handed it to me. She even told me how to get there from the store.

24 BAGGAGE AT THE TRUNK SHOW

The Florida sun was shining brightly on the morning of the Shop & Save Trunk show, and the temperature was a crisp fifty-eight degrees. Frankie was already up and gliding around the house when Cindy and Arnold joined in. Although Frankie moved busily about, she was completely at ease and in her element. Anyone could see that throwing parties was second nature for her.

Arnold and Cindy began spreading out scarves, purses, sweaters, jewelry and even shoes in designated areas around the house. Arnold had spent a lot of money on the inventory and was crossing his fingers that it would be a gamble that paid off. The "good news" was all of his customers had been buzzing about the show for weeks.

Around noon, Frankie, Arnold and Cindy meticulously surveyed the house, and ended up with an agreed upon feeling of satisfaction. Everything was in order. The dressing rooms would be set up shortly and that would be the final task. When the doorbell rang, Frankie jumped up to answer it. Johnny and Trenton walked in. Trenton let out a low whistle as he looked around.

"Some place you got here, Frankie!"

"Why thank you, Trenton." She motioned them into the kitchen. "Trenton, I was wondering if you would help Arnold set up the table in the dining room. I'm going to use it as a bar, and it just needs to be moved in front of the window there."

"Sure thing!" he said, with a little more excitement in his voice than intended. Arnold blushed and followed him into the dining room.

"Johnny, come on in here and meet my roommate, Cindy."

As Johnny rounded the corner, he was stunned by Cindy's pretty face. He seemed a bit taken aback, as he looked back at Frankie.

"Your roommate?" he asked. It seemed a little strange to have such a young roommate, but he wasn't complaining that someone so pretty lived next door.

"Yes, my roommate. Cindy, this is Johnny. He lives next door."

They shook hands. "Cindy, why don't you give Johnny the grand tour of the house? After he's familiar with everything, the two of us will go get beautiful!"

Then, Frankie turned to Johnny and said, "I can't thank you enough for helping out today!" As he followed Cindy to the stairs, he thought, *I should be thanking you!*

"Johnny," Frankie called out after him, "I do hope that you and Trenton will join us tonight. If shopping isn't your thing, I promise good food and a bustling bar!"

"Sounds great!" he called out after her.

***

Frankie took a step back and looked in the mirror. She smiled and a single tear slipped down her cheek. For the first time in a long time, she saw the old Frankie staring back. She had chosen a beautiful black dress from Arnold's collection. Putting on the diamond earrings Ed had given her for their first wedding anniversary, she smiled as she thought about the years they'd spent together. She recognized, though, she was now in a new chapter of her life. It was a new party, one full of both life and hope.

As Frankie walked down the stairs, she saw that the dress Arnold pulled for Cindy was perfect. He knew his stuff. The pale blue fabric hung to her curves in just the right places. She immediately noticed, too, she wasn't the only one who thought the dress was perfect. Johnny hadn't left the house all day, except for the few minutes it took him to shower and change for the party. Now he stood in the kitchen, staring at Cindy with a look of longing in his eyes.

Arnold walked over to Frankie and hugged her. "We're ready," he said. Trenton walked over with a tray of champagne glasses.

"How about a toast?" he said, as he passed the tray around. "To Frankie, one lady who knows how to have fun, to Johnny, my best friend and partner in crime, to Cindy, the sweet Midwestern girl who every man dreams of, and to Arnold, one of the sexiest men I've ever met."

Johnny choked on the sip of champagne he had been swallowing and looked at Trenton.

"I know, buddy. You didn't know. I've been wanting to tell you for a while, but then you had your accident . . . and I didn't want you to think about anything else but getting well. But, I've been feeling this way for a while . . . about men, I mean. I just wasn't sure how to let everyone know. Including Arnold."

They all turned to look at Arnold, who was now beet red. Everyone seemed frozen in time. Nobody said a word. Frankie, sensing the awkwardness spreading through the room, did what a good hostess always does—she took a sip of her drink, motioned for the band on the back porch to begin playing, and grabbed Arnold for a dance.

"Are you okay?" she asked him, once they were out on the floor dancing.

"Oh, um, I guess so." His eyes wandered around the backyard and then over at Trenton, who remained standing next to Johnny and Cindy. "Y'know, it's interesting. I guess I never really liked girls. I just thought it was because they didn't like me. Maybe I was just confused. I'm not sure what to think right now, Frankie."

"Well, right now, you have a life full of friends. Whether or not you and Trenton envolve into more, only time will tell. Right now, just enjoy the party!" She kissed him on the cheek, just as the doorbell rang and their first customer entered.

Frankie's house was soon full of Shop & Save customers trying on clothes, enjoying cocktails and chatting happily. Arnold had become a pro at sizing up what might look good on a customer. He was selecting dresses for some of the shoppers and suggesting scarves and necklaces for others. Cindy was moving from room to room, complimenting the women as they tried on the merchandise.

Everything was going along smoothly, until Cindy answered the door and was met by a woman in tears, who was demanding to speak with the manager of Shop and Save. Cindy tried to deflect the situation by offering the woman a cocktail and showing her to the living room to survey the jewelry. The woman declined the drink and the jewelry. Then, she began crying even harder. Still, after grabbing a handkerchief from her pocket and blowing her nose loudly, and then wiping her eyes and face unceremoniously with it, she gathered herself enough to face Cindy again, this time with more composure.

"Look, I just drove a long way to see the manager of Shop and Save. I drove for nine hours straight, and I ain't stoppin' now to look at jewelry or have me a drink. Just tell me where he is!"

As Frankie heard the commotion, she walked into the foyer and promptly put her arm around the young lady. "Follow me, I'll help you find him," she said. "Now where did you say you were from?"

"That ain't important. I just want to know, is he here or has he already gone to the Dominican Republic?"

"Honey, let's you and I walk into the back and get you cleaned up. The manager is here, and I assure you that he hasn't gone to the Dominican Republic."

Grace followed Frankie to the bathroom, where she was soon handed a wet cloth to wipe her face. Frankie quietly eyed Grace, wondering about how to proceed. As they walked out of the bathroom, both women nearly ran right into Arnold.

"I was looking for you," he said to Frankie. "Cindy told me somebody was asking for me."

Grace looked up at Arnold. "I want to know where Wayne is. He stole my money. He conned me. I want to see him . . . now!"

Arnold looked at the small woman with a perplexed expression. Other shoppers were beginning to gather around to find out what the excitement was about. Frankie nodded to the bartender and clapped her hands.

"Shoppers, we've got a special drink for you. It's called the Shopper's Shot. Enjoy!" Waiters promptly appeared with trays full of shots, and the inquisitive women were easily distracted. Within moments, they all wandered back to the display tables, shot glasses in hand.

Frankie motioned for Arnold and Grace to follow her. They walked through the house into a guest bedroom . Cindy, Johnny and Trenton followed them into the room too, just in case they needed support. Frankie shut the bedroom door. She looked at the poor, tired-looking woman.

"Now Mrs.- . . . um, what shall I call you?"

"Grace."

"Mrs. Grace."

"No, just Grace."

"Okay, Grace," Frankie began. "This is Arnold, the manager of the Shop & Save. What can we help you with?"

"Arnold?" she asked. "Where is Charles? Charles is the manager."

Arnold shook his head, somewhat relieved. "Charles, or Chuck," he answered, "doesn't work at the Shop and Save anymore. He was fired, and I took his place."

Grace's face fell. A split second later, so did her body. She collapsed onto the floor. Trenton bent down and carefully picked her up, placing her on the bed. The five friends looked at each other. Even Frankie seemed to be at a loss.

Cindy knelt down in front of Grace and took her hand. "It's okay, Grace. Don't cry. Whatever it is, we can help you figure it out. Why don't you tell us what happened."

Grace looked around at the room full of strangers. Nothing in her life seemed sacred anymore. Her love life, her prayers, her happiness. It was all over.

"I don't even know what happened. I don't know what to do. God has forsaken me. I thought He listened to me."

"Who?" Cindy asked.

"God," she answered as tears began streaming down her face. " I thought he loved me and heard my prayers. I even charge people for prayers, because I always thought I had God's ear. But I aint' got nothin'. I'm a fraud. Now, Wayne stole my money and took my heart. And to think, I was gonna' have sex with him."

Everyone in the room stood frozen, wondering what in the world to do with this woman crying on the bed. Cindy reached up and wiped the tears falling from Grace's eyes.

"God still hears you," she said. "Please believe that. I was in your place just a few weeks ago and look at where I am now. I have friends and a home in Florida, far away from tornadoes."

Grace stared at Cindy. "In Florida, far away from tornadoes? Is that what you said? Where are you from?"

"Oh, a little town called Humboldt."

Grace sucked in her breath. "I know you. You're Cindy."

Now it was Cindy's turn to be confused. She looked at Grace. "How do you know my name?"

"Did you pay someone online to pray for you?"

Cindy nodded, with her brows furrowed.

"I'm the prayer lady you pay to pray for you. You won your float contest and now you're in Florida."

"How did you find me? I don't understand."

"I didn't come to find *you*. I came to find *Wayne*. You just happened to be here." She shook her head. "*Humph!* Never figured *that* would happen."

Frankie knelt down next to Cindy and stared into Grace's eyes. "Grace? Have you ever prayed for parties?"

With that, Grace stood up from the bed and quickly made her way to the door. "I don't understand what's going on here! How did you know that?"

"Well, I'll be damned!" Frankie exclaimed. She turned to Cindy. "I was feeling real blue a few months back. I missed the life I used to share with my husband. I missed the parties we threw and were invited to. And one day, I ran across an internet ad for a prayer lady. I asked her to pray that I would have parties again. *And now look at me!* Throwing one of the most wonderful parties I've ever thrown, with some of the best friends I've ever had!"

She ran to Grace and threw her arms around her neck. "It was your prayers that did this, Grace! Don't you see?!"

With that, Arnold sat on the edge of the bed with a soft thud. "You're not going to believe this, but I think you might be *my* prayer lady, too! Absolution ring a bell?" he asked.

Grace nodded her head in astonishment.

"Well, hell!" boomed Trenton. "This is some *wild shit!* I don't suppose you've been praying for someone to find the face he saw in a vision, have you?"

With that, the whole room fell silent. Grace looked at the faces of the strangers staring at her. *Could it possibly be that all these people are clients of mine?*

Frankie walked over to the small sofa, sat down and patted the cushion. "Come on over here and sit down, Grace. Let's see if we can figure all of this out." Grace sat down, but made sure not to sit too close to Frankie. She felt like she was in an old episode of *The Twilight Zone*. Everyone else took a seat and, one-by-one, they shared their stories with each other, including Grace. When she finished telling them about giving her money to Wayne, they understood why she seemed so hurt and frail.

"I know Chuck," Arnold said. "I worked for him for four years. He was a con-man himself. He slept with many of the women out there shopping. Makes sense that someone like him and Wayne would be cousins."

"Well," Frankie said, "you are going to have to just move on, Grace. No use crying over spilt milk or a two-timing good for nothing like that. You've got *us,* now. Like it or not. It was your prayers and your faith that put us all here. God hasn't left you *at all.* He was just leading you in a different direction than you imagined you'd be going in."

Grace felt as if her heart would burst. *Frankie's right,* she thought. *How could I have doubted my faith? God has given Frankie parties, brought Cindy to Florida, helped Arnold embrace his life without guilt, and . . .*

She stopped and faced Johnny, looking at him squarely in the eyes. "Have you found your face?"

"No, I haven't. But I'm hoping I found more than just a face." He answered with a smile, as he glanced at Cindy.

"Well," started Frankie. "This calls for a celebration. Cindy, if you don't mind, can Grace here change in your room?

"Sure."

"I've got the perfect thing for you to wear," Arnold cut in. "I've got to get back to the shoppers, but Cindy, why don't you grab the pink sweater in the study."

Cindy looked at Johnny. "Would you mind showing Grace to my room? I'll be right up."

Johnny nodded and helped Grace up. "Right this way," he said. Johnny led her up the stairs and into the bedroom at the end of the hallway. "You'll feel much better after changing," he reasoned. As they waited for Cindy, Johnny walked over to the window. He noticed a small picture frame on the nightstand. He picked it up and looked at it, holding it out in front of the lamplight. With that, he sat on the bed and clutched the frame to his heart.

"You okay?" Grace asked.

"I thought Trenton was wasting his money paying you. I thought you were a fraud, but you *found* her," he said, handing the picture over to Grace. At that moment, Cindy walked in.

Johnny looked at her. "This is *her*. This is the woman I saw the night of my accident. It's *her!*"

Cindy walked over and took the picture. "Johnny, this is my *mother*. She died when I was born."

Grace nodded her head and began to feel as if all was right in the world again. "She's your guardian angel- and Cindy's too. She knew you were meant to be together." Grace turned to Johnny. "She knew you had to survive the accident. She was right there to help you through it- for her daughter. She knew Cindy here would need you."

Cindy began crying, as she looked from her mother's picture to Johnny. "Are you sure this was her?" she asked in a frail voice.

"Yes," Johnny said, "but her hair was curly."

25 GOD WORKS IN MYSTERIOUS WAYS

Dear God,

You sure work in mysterious ways. Even though it's been a rough day, I'm okay now. I should never have doubted that you was watchin' after me. It sure took a lot of fancy footwork to get me to see that you was right with me. Only you could have made the miracle of today happen. I think I found some good folks who are gonna be my friends for a long time. Thank you for Frankie, Arnold, Cindy, and Johnny. By the way, Dear Lord, I know that forgiveness is what I should be aimin' for, but I hope you think about punishin' Wayne, just a little, for what he put me through. In Jesus Christ's name I pray, Amen.

26 EPILOGUE

Frankie's house was filled with blue balloons and white roses. The smell of baked ham and rolls wafted through the air. Lullabies were playing over the speakers. Arnold held up a champagne glass and tapped it lightly with a spoon. However, the laughter and chatter was so loud that the sound was lost. Trenton stood on a chair next to Arnold and whistled loudly with his thumb and pointer finger held between his lips. This gesture got everyone's attention and silence fell over the room. Trenton stepped off the chair and winked at Arnold who was standing to his side. In a grand motion, he swept his arms toward Arnold, giving him the floor.

Adjusting his collar and sweeping his hand through his hair, Arnold thanked Trenton and cleared his throat. He had a tanned glow and highlights, which looked completely natural, but were the work of Leo, who sat staring admiringly across the room.

"I want to take a minute to toast Cindy, who is one of the most lovely women I've ever had the pleasure of meeting. She walked into the Shop and Save seven months ago, and every day since then, has only gotten better and better. She has shown me what a true friend can be. I promise to take my duties as your baby boy's godfather very seriously. He'll never be alone and he'll never be a fashion disaster, as I once was!"

The crowd clapped and drank from their glasses. Trenton playfully put his arm around Arnold, but kissed him sweetly on the cheek. Then Trenton held his glass toward Cindy. "I, too, promise to be the best godfather I can be. I'll make sure he has the starring role in one of my major motion pictures. I'll also teach him to throw the football better than anyone else in this room," he said, as he smiled at Johnny. "To the little guy!" he said, with tears welling in his eyes.

With that, Johnny stood and patted Trenton on the back. Then he turned to face Cindy. "Cindy, my life almost ended on a dark lonely road. Luckily for me, forces out of my control moved me to keep living. I'll never really understand the events of that night, but I will never doubt I am right where I'm supposed to be. Right here with my friends and family, and right here with you."

Walking across the room to Cindy, Johnny knelt down in front of her. He pulled a box from his pocket and opened it, revealing a beautiful engagement ring. Placing the ring on her finger, he reached his hands up and placed them on Cindy's stomach. "Cindy, will you and this little baby boy have me as a husband and father?"

Cindy blinked back tears, as she gazed into Johnny's eyes. She tried to speak, but nothing came. All she could manage was a nod, as she threw her arms around Johnny's neck. Cheers roared up from all around the room.

On the sofa, Nancy elbowed Ricky. "Did you know about this? You better not have!"

"Of course, I did," he answered. "Johnny is a gentleman. He asked me for her hand weeks ago."

"Ricky, I can't believe you kept this quiet!" She reached over and hugged him, as they watched Cindy and Johnny in each other's arms.

Frankie stood and motioned for the waiters. "This deserves another round of champagne," she said, beaming. "Cindy and Johnny, I couldn't be happier for you two. I know your lives will be filled with love and happiness. I only ask one thing from you both . . . I want to throw the engagement party, and the bridal shower, and the wedding *and* the Christening party, and whatever other parties you have!"

"Frankie," Cindy replied, "not only would we be honored to have you throw our parties for us, we would be *crushed* if you didn't. You're a part of our *family*,"

Frankie took a big swallow of her champagne. "What do you say we get to the dancing?" she asked.

But before she could signal the band to start the music, Grace raised her hand. She had been sitting quietly, enjoying herself as the party unfolded, but now, she felt like she needed to say something.

"I know you all want to get to dancin', but I hate not to make a toast myself. I want you to know I ain't ever been as honored as I was when you asked me to be your little baby's godmother, Cindy. That's a mighty big responsibility, which I promise to take on with my whole heart. I may live a ways away, but I promise to visit often. And even though you may not see me every day, know that I'm prayin' every day . . . for this special baby, and for all of ya'll."

After another round of cheers, the music began, and the party moved to the back porch, where everyone hit the dance floor.

***

Chuck popped open two bottles of beer and handed one to Drew. The sun was setting and three young women walked by in skimpy bikinis. Drew winked, as Chuck whistled. The girls shot a quick smile their way and continued down the beach.

"I told you, *paradise*," Chuck said.

"You were right, cousin," Drew answered. Went through enough shit to get here, but it was worth it!"

They each sat on a lounge chair and put their feet up. Drew took a deep breath and started to relax. As he swallowed a sip of beer, he scratched his head. It had become second nature. He had been plagued with lice since he had arrived in the Dominican Republic. He had tried medicated shampoos, natural remedies, the works—even the town witch doctor was at a loss. No matter what he did, they kept coming back. He scratched his head raw nearly every day. However, after a few beers, it became a little more bearable. So he sat, as he did most nights, watching the sun go down and clawing at his scalp.

Keep Reading For A Preview of Ashley's Next Book!

According to the Santalese Tribe in India, the sun God, Thakur Jew, is connected to the earth by an invisible vine that keeps him from floating away into the "all covering black." Each morning, Thakur Jew climbs to the top of the vine and tries to break free so that he will no longer be a prisoner. After spending the whole day attempting to escape, he is so exhausted that he falls back to the earth and his light goes out. The Santalese believe that the moment the sun god breaks the vine, the all covering black will take over the world and it will end. In an effort to convince Thakur Jew to enjoy his perch high atop the world and become content, each member of the tribe performs a ritual upon rising every morning. They tie their foot to a post in front of their hut with a piece of twine to mimic Thankur Jew's connection to the earth. After the rope is secure, they sing the Happy Earth song all the while smiling with their mouths and their hearts. The Santalese hope that Thakur Jew will take notice of their joy and begin to look at his capture as a blessing instead of a curse.

Maxfield Qaletaqa Akshay Ammon Keefe Jones gently untangled the sheet from around his arm. It was warm in the house and beads of sweat were gathered on his forehead. He wiped the drool from his cheek with the sheet and ever so carefully placed his feet on the floor. He glanced over his shoulder, and thankfully Alice was still asleep.

Maxfield's bladder seemed ready to burst, but in his small house, the flush from the toilet would surely wake Alice. He would have to hold it until he was finished with the song. He shifted his boxer shorts uncomfortably to make room for the erect penis that was nearly bursting because he had to urinate so bad.

He walked into the back yard and grabbed the exercise band that hung on the rusted lawn chair. He velcroed it around his ankle and placed the hand grip over the horseshoe stake that had been used for an actual horseshoe game last week with two of his buddies from the deli. He had never used it for its intended purpose before, but after a few beers and a couple of games with Sal and Ben, he decided that it would now have two uses in his life.

The sun was peering over his roof, and Maxfield could tell that it was going to be another scorching day in Alabama. He was still sweating and his erection was almost unbearable. So, he placed a big smile on his face and began to sing:

Oh, it is such a beautiful day,
The earth is filled with glorious ways.
Water to cool and flowers to smell,
Birds to sing and mankind to smile.
Happy am I to be a part of this happy earth!

Alice thought she heard Maxfield get out of bed. It was always awkward to wake up from a one night stand. She thought that she would wait until he left the room to get up. Then she could throw on her clothes so that he wouldn't see the cellulite rippled bottom. After a few martinis, that bottom turned into the rock-hard ass she had in college, at least in her mind. As soon as he left the room, she grabbed her tee-shirt and jeans and put them on as quickly as possible.

She walked into the small kitchen that overlooked the back yard and saw Maxfield. He was standing in the middle of his yard tied to a stake with his penis pointing straight through the hole in his boxer shorts. He had a goofy smile on his face and was singing something. She couldn't make out the words, but she didn't need to. She knew that he had to be a psychopath or kinky sex freak. She had seen Silence of the Lambs and Psycho. She wasn't staying around to see if Maxfield favored Hannibal or Norm. She grabbed her keys and bolted for the front door.

Maxfield heard the car start and muttered, "shit!" under his breath. However, he kept a big smile on his face until he took the band off his ankle. He let out a sign and relieved himself on the ligustrum hedge that grew along the fence.

It had been almost six months since he had been caught singing the Happy Earth song. He could usually make it to the yard and back while his lady friend was sleeping. On the occasion that he was seen, the women absolutely refused to listen when he tried to explain his predicament.

The opposite sex has become so skeptical, he thought. *How does anyone find a girlfriend, much less a wife?* he wondered.

But there wasn't much time to think about that now.

About the Author

Ashley lives in Jacksonville, Florida with her husband,Don, and her children Savannah, Trip, Cole and Piper. Comin' Across Grace is her first completed work of fiction. Her quirky writing style is largely influenced by her southern upbringing.

Ashley has a strong passion about her religion; however, she believes deep in her heart, that God has a wonderful sense of humor and wants us to live a life where laughter and joy outweigh guilt and sorrow.

She is currently working on her second novel.